A LITTLE BIT BRITISH

Is there anything *funny* about the Ulster situation?
 Heaven forbid! (both *Heavens*)
 A Little Bit British is not the whole truth about Ulster in the violent month of August 1969. It is a private part of the truth (Augustus Harland's very private, never previously published diary, to be precise). It is concerned with what people believed to be happening, whether it happened or not. It is a story of ... well, having got this far you should sit down quietly and read this little masterpiece by the highly talented author of **Otley**.

It *is* a funny book.

It is also an *unpleasant* book, if you want to take it like that.

Look before you laugh.

Martin Waddell is a little bit British and a little bit Irish as well. Born in 1941, he lives and writes in his native province. His marriage to a Roman Catholic confused the Ulster Presbyterian in his bones and, perhaps, foreshadows the ultimate solution of the Irish problem. Educated mainly in England, Martin Waddell drew on his knowledge of the London street markets for his quartet of **Otley** novels (... *a natural comedy writer*—Times Literary Supplement ... *unstoppably readable*—The Sun), one of which was successfully filmed. He has written a novel about drunken Belfast **Come Back When I'm Sober** (... *a blessed irreverence*—The Irish Times), and numerous short stories, in addition to pieces for radio and television.

Neither of his countries understands him.

by the same author

OTLEY
OTLEY PURSUED
OTLEY FOREVER
OTLEY VICTORIOUS

and, about Belfast:

COME BACK WHEN I'M SOBER

A LITTLE BIT BRITISH

being the diary of an Ulsterman, August 1969

MARTIN WADDELL

TOM STACEY LTD

Tom Stacey Ltd.,
Editorial Office: 28 Maiden Lane, London W.C.2
Trade Counter: 11a Stratford Road, London W.8

First published 1970

Copyright © Martin Waddell

SBN 85468 016 0

Printed in Great Britain by
Northumberland Press Limited
Gateshead

A LITTLE BIT BRITISH

It has now become impossible for British citizens resident in Northern Ireland to accept the obligations inherent in that citizenship and, at the same time, uphold the present Unionist administration.

Mr Harland ... whose diary this is ... would not see it that way. Mr Harland is one of those thinly disguised extremists who turn up in every trouble spot, pronouncing themselves to be moderate men of good sense. I believe that, in the Northern Ireland context, Mr Harland, although to some extent a gross figure, represents the feelings, spoken or unspoken, of many British citizens who are not prepared to live up to their obligations to the Crown and Constitution in which they take so great a pride. He would be as great a bigot anywhere he happened to set foot, be it South Africa, Germany, or either of the Georgias ... Soviet or American.

I am indebted to the *Belfast Telegraph* and the *Belfast Newsletter* for much of the material used in writing this book. Where real people are quoted, the quotes are those which appeared in these two papers. In no instance have I knowingly used any real person or incident side by side with a fictitious event without making the distinction between the quotation and Harland's commentary implicit. All headlines are those which appeared in the papers on the appropriate days, and Harland's interpretation of events is not intended to reflect in any way on the papers concerned.

> Martin Waddell,
> Donaghadee,
> Co. Down,
> Northern Ireland.
> September 1969

FRIDAY, FIRST OF AUGUST

A red letter day ... my birthday. August the first. The First Day of Augustus Harland, as my father used to say. Father was a wonderfully amusing man, and I am happy to say that I have inherited his keen sense of humour. August the First is my birthday, and also the birthday of this little book, a gift from my daughter Angelica Elizabeth, and the occasion of a touching exchange between us.

Here is Angelica's letter (sent with the book) in full:

> St Matthew's Hospital,
> Warden Lane,
> Stockwell.
> 29/7/69

Dear Daddy Augustus,

Many happy returns of your day! I will be thinking of you all, Daddy Augustus, Mummy Victoria, Grandmother Gertie and the absent fiend, my dear brother Craig, as you gather around the table at 12 Boyne Villas this morning for your Birthday Binge.

I am afraid that Matron was quite unable to release me this year in time to return for Your Day. I was frightfully upset, but Matron was adamant, and I am sure you would not wish me to desert my post in the face of the enemy. Tell Mummy Victoria it is *hard labour* here.

Dear Daddy Augustus, the enclosed little book in its red white and blue binding is for you to set down your Loyal thoughts in, so that they may be recorded

for posterity. I am sure that posterity will get more out of them then your off-spring,
                    Angelica Elizabeth.

I am not ashamed to say that my wife Victoria Alberta and I regard this letter as healing the breach between us and our little stray lamb.

'It is over, Victoria,' I said, as I handed the note to my dear wife. When she had finished reading it, she raised her eyes (concealed by dark glasses owing to misuse of our sun ray lamp in an attempt to gain an Autumn tan) to meet mine, and we smiled at each other. 'You see,' I said simply, 'we were right.' Then I went to the desk in the front parlour and wrote a simple note to my daughter straight from the heart of a firm but fond parent.

Here it is, in full. (I am determined that this little book shall know all):

12 Boyne Villas,
Belfast.
August 1st., 1969

Dear Sweetening,

Your Mummy Victoria and I were delighted to receive your letter and the lovely gift. We hope that now the fire and thunder twixt us is o'er you will once more return to Boyne Villas and be enjoined with us, Back in the Bosom of Your Home.
                    Your Daddy Augustus.
P.S. We have not heard from Craig for some weeks, but he has been to dinner with a Senator. You may be proud of your brother.
P.P.S. There is a Blackie Doctor in the Royal Victoria Hospital. Your Mummy Victoria was quite terrified of him, and insisted on being brought home.

What a happy day!

The sun shone through my window this morning, straight across our twin beds. My dear wife stirred in her sleep as I lay and counted my blessings, which are manifold.

I have all my faculties, although I do wear glasses when reading. I am blessed with two wonderful children and a gracious wife, a Happy Home and a Heart Full of the Goodness of the LORD. I am a Loyal Ulsterman, a Briton through and through. I am an able administrator, I make no bones about that, and my toil has found its reward in the outer office of Blaney, Aiken and McMaster where I have recently been appointed under-manager. I am a founder member of U.M.P.I.R.E. (Ulster Moderate Protestant Inter-Religious Educationalists) and I have several times had my name mentioned in the *Belfast Telegraph* in connection with Community Projects, following the lead of Captain O'Neill. (He was, I am assured, badly misled by the Other Side, but he did his duty as an officer and a Protestant gentleman, and I am proud to say that I played my part. If only the other side had not let us down. It is like the Blackies my son Craig has to cope with. These people are never satisfied with what you give them.) Nevertheless I think that mine is not a bad record for a humble man, although I say it myself.

My Birthday is always the occasion of some festivity in Our Little Home. I believe that no man should be wholly adult, too far above the Baba within him to allow for a little simple joy. Jesus saith: 'Suffer the Little Children to Come Unto Me' and I am persuaded by my reading of the Gospels that he meant the Children of Innocence. Thus on My Birthday and other Great Days of family festivity I gather my little brood together in the front room of the Home and we make merry, putting our day by day cares behind us. We have crackers, paper-hats, and a special cake baked by

Mother. (Who is allowed to potter around in the kitchen by the Matron at the Home). We are a small family, my wife Victoria Alberta, our daughter (already mentioned) Angelica Elizabeth, our Son Craig (Who is now in the United States of America, in California, where he is rapidly becoming a person of some importance. Craig is a veterinary surgeon. He is a great joy to me). It is my custom to bring Mother across town on these occasions, with her cake. I feel, and Victoria Alberta has come to agree with me, that Mother should share in all our little ceremonies, which bring the family so much closer together. It also pleases mother to be taken out of the Gentlefolks Home every so often, and means that on the week-end following the festival day we can fore-go our usual visit, as too much excitement is not good for her.

After breakfast, when Victoria Alberta had read our Sweetening's letter and I had penned my reply, I took the car out of the garage and went across town for Mother, stopping off at Mr Bingham's for my morning *Newsletter*.

There was an unpleasant incident in Mr Bingham's shop. I was standing by the counter with him discussing the unpleasant happenings in Hooker St. ... some Roman Catholic Louts (Loots, I call them) had been causing trouble again ... when a young man in a leather jacket tapped Mr Bingham on the shoulder. He wanted a copy of the *Morning Star*.

Mr Bingham was splendid. 'I'm afraid we don't stock your long haired socialist muck here!' he exclaimed.

The young man went away with a flea in his ear.

'Well done, Bingham,' I said, slapping him heartily on the shoulder.

'We have enough trouble with the R.C.s,' Bingham said. 'We can do without Socialist riff-raff hanging around our necks. When Communist newspapers are openly on sale in our streets, it makes one think. See where your Moderate Administration has got us, Harland.'

Bingham is not the most moderate of men. Right from the start he was critical of the way the Captain was leading us, though latterly he has expressed himself as satisfied with the regime of Major Chichester-Clark. But I must confess that I do consider that a closer watch should be kept upon the peddling of open revolution and anarchy in our streets.

'Something will have to be done about this sort of thing,' I said.

'Not only that,' said Bingham, and he went behind the counter and came back with an astounding little booklet. 'There you are, Harland,' he said. 'Take that and study it!'

He handed me a small illustrated booklet entitled *Garter-Girl*.

'It makes one wonder,' I said, flicking through the pages.

'She has big'uns, hasn't she?' said Bingham.

'Bordering upon deformity,' I said. 'I am shocked to learn that illustrations of this nature are on sale in our city.'

'Well,' said Bingham. 'I have said all along that this is where all this talk of Anarchy and Revolution would lead us. Roman Communists like Fitt are raising the rabble with this muck!' I was happy he had said this, because it allowed me to step in with one of my jokes.

'You don't mean rabble-rousing, Mr Bingham,' I said. 'No indeed. What you mean is *rebel*-rousing!'

Mr Bingham thought this was very good, and so did Mother, when I told it to her in the car coming back for our little festivity. Not that one should joke about these things, when such vileness is allowed to pollute the streets of our Protestant City. My dear Father who turned out with Craig and Carson in Ulster's finest hour would have turned in his grave if he'd seen the muck Bingham showed me.

I shall write to the *Newsletter* about it.

I am afraid that our little celebration was not altogether a success. In the first place, owing to the absence of my daughter Angelica Elizabeth (At her post in London) and my son Craig (Now doing very well in California) our little party was but a sad shadow of the usual merry band which gathers round the old jo-anna in the sitting-room for our celebrations, though of course our dear ones were very much with us in spirit. (And ... most unfortunately, in spirits!)

Perhaps I should explain that I am not a drinking man myself, but I am not one to deprive an old age pensioner of her little pleasures and I know that Mother (Although Father would *not* have approved) has recently become partial to alcoholic refreshment. In confidence, I have heard it said that Mrs McGrath, the resident Matron at the Gentlefolks, is not all she ought to be in matters of sobriety, and I very much fear that she may have been leading Mother astray. Whatever the cause, I felt it incumbent upon me to provide a small bottle of sherry for our blow out, which Victoria Alberta purchased for me at an off licence in the supermarket. It was South African, and the man assured Victoria Alberta that it was good value for money, though to my mind any money spent on liquor is money down the drain, or gold down the gullet as I aptly phrased it. However, Victoria Alberta agreed that Mother should have her little drink, and we set out the sherry for her, alongside our glasses (we were drinking ginger wine).

We blew out the candles and joined hands to sing Happy Birthday Dear Daddy Augustus (normally I would not have joined in, but as the children were absent I felt that I could safely do so, representing them as it were by proxy, and keeping up the spirit of the thing) and Victoria Alberta (in the unavoidable absence of our son Craig, the Veterinary Surgeon) proposed a toast to my health. Mother, who was a little over excited by this time, a reaction which I attributed to the pleasure of being in our Home once more, responded to this toast somewhat incoherently.

'What was that, Mother?' said Victoria Alberta (Whose ears are sharper than mine, owing to my exposure to noise waves in the Blitz as an officer of the A.R.P. based on East Belfast, a war injury which had yet to be recognized in £.s.d. by the Military Authorities, despite repeated appeals through my Member of Parliament).

'Old arse-face always falls on his bum,' said Mother, downing her sherry at a gulp, and eyeing us defiantly.

'Really Mother,' I said, more concerned for her than hurt by her slighting remark. (Mother has always been more outspoken than the rest of the family, although when Father was alive she scarcely spoke a word.) 'Do you consider that a suitable remark to make in front of Victoria Alberta?'

'Silly Cow!' said Mother, swaying slightly.

'She's drunk,' snapped Victoria Alberta, drawing herself up (She is a splendid figure of a woman. Our son Craig has inherited his carriage from his mother, and his brain and ready wit from my branch of the family tree. I am a man of moderate stature ... moderate, indeed, in all things.)

'Crap!' exclaimed Mother, stepping back.

'Mother!' I cried, springing forward towards her, and inadvertently spilling my ginger wine down my Ulster tie. At that moment Mother somehow managed to lose her balance, and fell backwards, striking her lower back against the screen of our television set, and shattering it.

Victoria Alberta left the room.

Mother started to cry.

I will draw a veil over the rest of a miserable evening. My day, which had begun so splendidly, was quite spoilt by the irresponsibility of others, to wit Mrs McGrath of the Gentlefolks, who had (Quite against my express instructions, and those of the Rev. Dunwoody) allowed my Mother to purchase a bottle of gin, on easy terms.

It is my intention to take this matter up with the Gentlefolks Committee, who contribute to Mrs McGrath's wage.

It appears that Mother's cake also contained an alcoholic ingredient. We have left it untouched.

SATURDAY, SECOND OF AUGUST

The last day of my holiday, a Saturday. (Sunday is, of course, God's day).

Mother has returned to the Gentlefolks, after a visit to Dr Faulkner. I am sorry to say that her injuries were quite serious, as the shattered screen of our television set had penetrated the fleshy parts of her lower back.

Our television set is damaged beyond repair. I took it to the Repair Shop, where a young man advised to me to purchase another, using the hire purchase system. I told him that this was little more than a licensed debt, and quoted the dictum. 'Neither a Borrower nor a Lender be.' The young man seemed to be surprised, and said I was, 'very old fashioned, everyone does it now'. I replied that this was perhaps why everyone was in such a sorry mess. Later I learned that his name was Delaney, which explains a lot. These people live on our family allowances and encourage each other to run up vast debts by living above their incomes. Why cannot the R.C.s live like decent Protestants?

I mentioned this exchange to Mr Bingham, when I was collecting my newspaper, and pointed out to him that these people would be lost without their allowances if they got their precious Republic. Mr Bingham agreed with me and told me of a family with eighteen children on the Falls Road, and the father out of employment.

'They'll find their Republic a bitter pill,' I joked, but unfortunately the effect of this was spoiled, as Mr Bingham was attending to a small child who wished to purchase a sweetmeat.

To be serious for a moment, it is a fact that these people are living off the backs of our business community and cannot, or will not, seek out a decent job. The New Ulster is a land of equal opportunity for all, and they know it. The Ulsterman is a decent chap, who knows what's what. Our Freedom is founded upon Our Protestant Faith, and if these R.C.s can't live within our community they should get out of it, and leave us to the real work of building the economy. They are just the same as those Asians in Birmingham or the Blackies in the States. My son Craig tells me that something will have to be done about the Blackies out there or they will take over everything, just as the R.C.s would like to do here. One may not agree with everything the Rev. Ian Paisley says (Though basically he is a good man, and what is more a brave outspoken man) but he is certainly right when he says that the R.C. Cardinal should come forward and openly avow that they accept our Protestant Constitution.

I was saying as much to Mr Bingham when a young man interrupted us. (It was, Bingham said, the same young man who had previously come in searching for Communist propaganda, about which I must remember to write to the *Newsletter*. Something should be done about that muck. While Good Men Stay Silent...) In any event, this young man had come to the counter, and was waiting to purchase a copy of the *Irish News* (An R.C. newspaper) which he had the effrontery to wave at Mr Bingham, as he exclaimed. 'The Cardinal has acknowledged the Constitution, several times.'

'Indeed,' said Mr Bingham, holding his temper very well. 'And when may we expect to see the Union Jack fly over Rome, pray?'

It was a brilliant sally, and the young man retreated in confusion.

Bingham is a good sort.

I am afraid that all is not well in 12 Boyne Villas. My wife, Victoria Alberta, has been of a nervous disposition since the birth of our youngest, Angelica Elizabeth, and I am afraid that the little fraças with Mother yesterday has been a bad setback to her. I must say that relations between Mother and Victoria Alberta have always been a matter of some concern to me. Victoria Alberta was brought up in a very refined household (Her Father was one of the Crosbie Porters of Banbridge. They were very firm in their Faith, and leaders of the local community). My own Father, a rare old character, dragged himself up by his boot strings, and I, for one, am not ashamed to say so. He had a hard and bitter struggle to become his own man, in the little shop on the Albertbridge road. His was a rich life, displaying the full tapestry of a rags to riches success story. He was a rough diamond, but in later years he was known to all as a fine old gentleman. When he died, his funeral (conducted from the Gentlefolks Home, where I had arranged for him to spend his Autumn years) was attended by representatives of all creeds (Protestant) and walks of life, a fine tribute to a great man, and a Christian. Be that as it may, I am afraid that Mother, though in many ways a kind and open hearted woman, never quite escaped from the defects of her early life and upbringing. She continued to associate with some quite unsuitable people from Rica Street long after Father had moved up in life, without thought for his position and the fact that he had the reputation of his business to consider. In later years this coarse element in my Mother has often given cause for offence, particularly to Victoria Alberta, and I am sorry to say that the incident of My Birthday Festivity was only one of many.

Victoria now says that Mother will not be admitted into our Home again.

I am bound to say that I sympathize with Victoria

Alberta, although I am constrained by what I consider to be my filial duty. I quite agree that Mother, by her behaviour, has sacrificed all right to be considered, and yet one has to think of the children, and the effect it might have upon them if there were talk in the neighbourhood. Angelica Elizabeth, in particular, has always been a favourite of Mother's, and might take badly to any suggestion which might be put about by ignorant persons that my Mother was not (as she is) enjoying the best of both worlds, with expert care and attention at the Gentlefolks, and regular cheering visits from her kith and kin. However, at present, Victoria Alberta is far too upset to discuss the matter and I am sure that, when she has recovered from our little unpleasantness, we will reach a sensible compromise.

As an Ulsterman, I think it worthy of note in my little book that today is the day of the Pop for Peace concert, an inter-denominational effort. (The organizers include, I understand, an R.C. priest, Father Marcellus, several prominent persons from our side (to stop him turning it into a *Pope* for Peace concert!!!!), and that arrogant Socialist and Labourite Patrick Devlin. (So this time they can hardly complain about discrimination, can they?)) I gather that several popular music bands (British!!!) have been invited to come over, and the organizers hope that the young people of Belfast will gather together and express a common purpose for peace. One could wish that this enterprise could have been undertaken without the aid of a man like Devlin (Devil'n!!!), who continues to plague our Prime Minister, Major James Chichester-Clark, with impudent and irrelevant questions relating to the Republican assault on the R.U.C. at Burntollet, and later (Quite blatantly) on the streets of Derry, when it was all our men could do to stop them proclaiming their R.C. Republic there and then. Devil'n (I shall continue to call him that) should consider where his Stormont salary comes from, not to mention his family allowance. He has a daughter, who is never happy except when making trouble. I do not know for a fact whether Devil'n is related to the Honourable Member for Mid Ulster, but I do know that he and the Communist R.C. Burn-a-debt (my own joke) are birds of a feather. Thank goodness we have men of determination and grit to resist them, just as good men everywhere resist the inroads of R.C. communistic anarchy. (My son Craig, though far from these shores, fights the same fight over there with the Blackies and the Jews). However, despite the unfortunate Devil'n and the mini-minded Burn-a-debt one cannot but hope that this new Pop for Peace Movement will succeed in showing the R.C.s the error of their ways.

God knows our Wee Ulster needs Peace.

I have written to the committee of U.M.P.I.R.E. (Ulster Moderate Protestants Inter-religious Educationalists) (of which I am a founder member) (One of my community projects, in response to Captain O'Neill's lead) recommending that we sponsor an Ulster Bands for Peace Concert, where the flute and other bands and marching organizations who perform so splendidly on Our Glorious Twelfth Day should hold a rally (preferably in Windsor Park) to play and march to the tunes of Ulster. Members of all denominations to be invited, and a Pledge to Our Constitution to be signed upon admittance. I cannot see that any right thinking person (Wherever they may attend Sunday Worship) could object to an entertaining and instructive afternoon such as this, where the old tunes would remind us of our common British Heritage (Protestant and Catholic) and the essential unity of our moderate people. I think it is initiatives of this sort which will one day lead us back along the paths of sanity unity under the Queen and Constitution and the Red, White and True Blue British Flag for which our forefathers fought.

I then wrote a letter which I believe to be worthy of note.

This is what I wrote:

> 12, Boyne Villas,
> Belfast,
> 2nd, August 1969.

Dear Editor,

As a moderately literate man (Moderate in all things) I should like to protest at the appalling socialist and communistic muck which is offered for sale all over Belfast. A publication of this nature has recently come into my hands and I am convinced the filth therein constitutes a threat to the minds of our children. I appeal to all moderate and reasonable Christian Ulstermen and Ulsterwomen to join with me in condemning this purveying of Communistic filth on the streets of our city. If interested readers would care to get in touch with me, we shall see what action right thinking people can take.

> I remain,
> At the convenience of the public,
> Yours,
> Augustus Harland (Ex-A.R.P.)

I made several copies of this letter, and despatched them to responsible journals. There comes a time when we must all stand up and be counted. I may say in passing that I have looked once more through the publication *Garter-Girl* and I am convinced that not all the charms displayed therein are God's unaided gifts. I have, however, resisted the temptation to burn *Garter-Girl*, as I shall require it for purposes of my campaign.

I have still had no word from my son Craig, the Veterinary Surgeon. He has obtained a good position in an animal cemetery in California, where he is in charge of a number of assistants (including Blackies).

Will the Westminster Government never act to stop this brain drain? Young men like Craig cannot reasonably be expected to forego the rewards awaiting their hard earned skills on the other side of the Atlantic. My son and I indulged in deep soul searching before the decision to go was reached, and I betray nothing that he would have me conceal when I say that we both regarded the matter as one which scorched us to the very steel of our blood. Craig is as British as the next man. I have brought him up to believe in our British Way of Life, and our Faith. I like to think that a little bit of our Empire spirit will be with him, where 'er he roams. But there you are! While our government slumbers, fine young men are lost to Britain, and Blackies get in. And all the while the rag tag and bobtail of the Bogside and Falls Road R.C. Hooligans sit on their backsides telling their beads and living off our family allowances.

I have had a brief phone call from Mother. I am afraid that she does not seem to be well. The Matron, Mrs McGrath, interrupted our conversation (mother had become incoherent) and demanded that I come to see her, forthwith. While I have no desire to interview the woman (Her behaviour is, so to speak, *sub judice* although I have not yet written to the Gentlefolks Committee) I suppose I had better go along and see what she has to say.

I must speak to Mother about using language on the telephone system. One can, I believe, be prosecuted.

William Fullerton, my next door but one neighbour, has just come to the door with the news that R.C. Hooligans have attacked an inoffensive and interdenominational parade of Junior Orange Lodges, which happened to be passing their flats at Unity Walk.

Will these people never stop?

I wonder what Captain O'Neill is thinking now? The spirit of communal activity, for which our ex-P.M.

struggled so long, lies shattered by the brickbats and socialist slogans of these mini mobsters.

I sincerely hope that the government will take steps to show these R.C.s that we won't put up with it much longer. I suggest that they be expelled from their luxurious council flats and Loyalist Citizens be moved in. That would teach them.

What I should like to know is: Who is going to foot the bill?

We ratepayers will not stand for much more of it.

I have sent a telegram to Cardinal Conway asking him, on behalf of the Loyalist Ratepayers of Belfast to issue a statement condemning R.C. Hooliganism. I have also sent one in Victoria Alberta's name.

If we Protestants can see things fairly and impartially, taking all sides into account before Jesus, why cannot the Other Side?

Must all we stand for be torn apart by Republican Rebels?

Where are the Moderate Men of Ulster? If we all banded together I am quite sure we could teach these extremists a lesson in the language they understand best ... a damn good thrashing all round, and cut off the family allowances!!!

SUNDAY, THIRD OF AUGUST

A most unfortunate day.

The Rev. Dunwoody, after church this morning, brashly invited himself to 12 Boyne Villas for Sunday Luncheon. I realized at once that something was amiss and, as soon as we were alone together in the front parlour, I taxed him with it. He then saw fit to read me the most extraordinary lecture, to such an extent that I have quite forfeited all the respect I once had for the man. The cloth has gone to his head. (Or perhaps his head is made of cloth!!!)

It appears that Mrs McGrath from the Gentlefolks has complained to the Committee about my Mother, and asked that she be removed from the Home forthwith. This without any further consultation with me!

'Please have the goodness to explain to me why?' I said, sitting by my own hearthside, and firmly keeping myself in my seat, though I felt sorely tempted to expel him there and then, Minister of Religion or not.

'Well, Mr Harland, my dear Augustus, it seems that your Mother ... (And here he paused and examined his fingernails in a most irritating manner before continuing) ... it seems that your Mother's behaviour of late has been ... ah ... distressing some of the other more retiring residents.'

'Indeed,' I said.

'We all know about your Mother's little weakness, of course,' he said.

'You may all know,' I said. 'I regret that I do *not* know.'

'Oh come now, Augustus,' he said, reprovingly.

'I am aware that Mother is accustomed to a little alcoholic refreshment now and then,' I said, straightforwardly. 'A vice ... if it be a vice in her case ... which, considering her advanced age, I feel one may excuse on medicinal grounds. I further understand that Mrs McGrath had taken steps to encourage Mother's drinking ... if that be the word ..: and the dear old lady herself has told me that Mrs McGrath accepts a commission on sales to the Gentlefolks from a local publican! (This was, perhaps, a slight exaggeration of what Mother had told me, but it would no doubt be borne out by investigation). 'However, be that as it may,' I said, 'my Mother is a person of probity, not given to undue excess in any field, and I am sure that she would never give such offence to others as you have given to me, and to the memory of my dear and Loyal Father, concerning whose Protestant Faith there was never any doubt.'

'It is not a matter of Faith, Augustus,' said the Rev. Dunwoody, uneasily.

'Indeed,' I said, scathingly. 'You think not, do you?'

He chose to ignore this and went on: 'Whatever the extent of your Mother's ... ah ... addiction to alcohol, Augustus, I fear that it is quite another matter which has caused Mrs McGrath to request that she be removed from the Gentlefolks.'

'Have the goodness to proceed,' I said.

'It is your Mother's ... ah ... political views which have been upsetting the other ... ah ... old persons.'

'Are they not Loyalists?' I cried. 'If my Mother is to be criticized in a Protestant Home run under the auspices of our authorities for expressing the basic true blue Loyalism which lies in her heart, a Loyalism which my dear Father, whose services to Queen and Crown I trust you will remember, in particular the Memorial lead roofing in your...'

He interrupted me, somewhat testily. 'We were speaking of your Mother, Augustus,' he said.

'Yes, indeed we were,' I said, not allowing myself to become flustered by the man's boorishness. 'If these lukewarm Loyalists at the Gentlefolks can't take the forthright statements of a woman who was present at the creation of our state, and marched hand in hand down the broad avenue of life with my Father, the flag before them, for many a long year, then I, for one, am ashamed of my church, and you in particular, Dunwoody. Obviously you have failed to counter the baleful influence of this woman McGrath, who has brought decadence to our old folk.'

'I am afraid that it is not your Mother's Loyalism which is at issue,' Dunwoody said. 'Rather the reverse, in fact.'

'What?' I said, quite mystified.

'I am sorry to say that your Mother has taken to abusing our leaders during their appearances on the communal T.V. in the Wakehurst Room at the Home. As this caused some irritation to other residents, Mrs McGrath was forced to restrict your mother's hours of viewing to the early afternoon.'

'Reverend Dunwoody,' I said, holding up my hand to stop him. 'Can you blame an old woman, a firm True Blue, from speaking out when she sees the lazy liberal line taken by our politicians? Bred, as she was, on the policies of No Surrender and the Gospel Doctrine based on the Book, can you wonder that she finds our present milk and water Protestantism a scurvy brew?'

'Apparently, Augustus, your dear Mother favours the removal of the border, and integration with the Irish Republic.'

To say I was stunned is to understate the matter. 'I do not believe you,' I said, finally.

'My dear Augustus,' said the Rev. Dunwoody. 'As your spiritual adviser I can see how difficult this must be for you. Old persons are sometimes subject to eccentric quirks, and I am sorry to say that in your mother's case this has taken the form of rejection of that system of British Democracy and Freedom for which your family has always stood.'

'A Republican!'

'I am sorry to say that that is now your Mother's view.'

'I do not believe it,' I said. 'My Mother has been misrepresented.'

At that moment Victoria Alberta came in, and we were forced to discontinue the conversation, as I did not wish to alarm my wife with false rumours about Mother.

After dinner, there was nothing for it ... to my mind ... but to make my way to the Gentlefolks Home and remove Mother from the care of that woman. Rev. Dunwoody came with me, and I think he understood from my rigid silence as we drove to the Home how sharply I disapprove of his conduct in relation to Mother and myself. Neither did I demean myself by arguing with Mrs McGrath, a low kind of woman, beneath one's contempt. Mother, I am happy to say, was her sweet old silver-haired self. I loaded her things into my car and drove her away, *unfortunately!!!!* neglecting to pick up the misbegotten Dunwoody ... I will not call him Reverend, for he is plainly not revered by me or mine.

I had planned to surprise Victoria Alberta with mother's arrival, but I am afraid that things did not go off at all well. My wife, flesh of my flesh, heart of my heart, even went so far as to bar the door to her own husband and his ageing parent.

'No, Augustus,' she said. 'I will not have that woman in here, reeking of alcohol.'

I pointed out to her that the front door of No. 12 was scarcely the place to dispute such an intimate matter, especially on the Lord's Day. Meanwhile

Mother, completely unaware that she was the cause of all this hubbub, sat waiting in the car.

'Victoria Alberta,' I said. 'I have been a good husband, in all senses of the word, to you, have I not? I have laboured in the vineyards. I have toiled for you with the sweat of my brow.'

'Your Mother,' she said, 'is not coming in.'

'As a Christian, Victoria Alberta...'

'That old bag is a savage,' she said, showing rare anger.

'Mother is not an old bag,' I said.

'Isn't she?' said Victoria Alberta. 'I have spoken to Mrs McGrath at the Home. I know all about her. Drinking and swearing and singing Republican songs. Setting up her own little barricades in the corridors, knocking down innocent old men ... and the language!'

I am afraid that I was forced to be firm with my wife, whilst chalking up another black mark against Mrs McGrath. I should not be surprised if she and Dunwoody have laid themselves open to a libel action, spreading false tales about Mother as they have done. It is, of course, not true that Mother blocked the corridors at the Gentlefolks Home, and set up her own barricades. This is, in fact, one of Mrs McGrath's gross distortions of the truth which is that a certain unpleasant old man, a Mr Castle, had been making advances upon her virtue, which the old lady understandably spurned. As to the accusations of Republicanism ... these are manifestly absurd. Mother, like the rest of us, knows which side her bread is buttered. Republicanism = ruination = Romanism, for Ulster Protestants. Our bread is buttered on the British side, and there can be no going back on that.

To cut a long story short I have managed to persuade Victoria Alberta to allow Mother the use of the attic ... though quite how she expects that frail old lady to climb the dangerous and shaky ladder I know not ... for a matter of a few days until I can get her fixed up in a suitable place.

I had some little difficulty getting Mother into the attic (disused since my son Craig ceased his studies there) and Victoria Alberta was not able to help, as she was indisposed, and went for a lie down. I am sorry to say that my son Craig, (usually the most hygienic of boys) had left some of his specimens in the attic and these had (with the passage of time) become a little rare. The ladder, as I had thought, produced some problems, as it folds down from the attic and is released by pulling upon a stout rope. Suffice it to say that the ladder broke, so long had it been out of use. Naturally I was able to fix it, but the problem now is that the ladder is perforce a semi-permanent structure, as the attic hinges have snapped. This leaves very little room for anyone to pass on either side and, as the ladder bars the door of the master bedroom, we shall have some slight inconvenience with it. It is a comparatively easy business to leave the master bedroom via the roof of the kitchen extension and pass into the yard below via a step ladder I have provided for the purpose. I am sorry to say that Victoria Alberta, when acquainted with the news of this innovation, did not receive it well. However, as it is at her insistence that Mother has been relegated to the attic, I have told her that she must learn to live with it.

Mrs Fullerton has complained about Mother singing in the attic. I am assured that Mother was singing Shirley Temple Oldies.

MONDAY, FOURTH OF AUGUST

Back to work! Hearty greetings from my workmates at Blaney, Aiken and McMaster, no doubt relieved to see me back at the outer office tiller once more.

While I have been away young Scullion has made an abominable mess of the monthly figures, as I expected he would. Perhaps that will teach them to go over my head and appoint young persons who lack both experience and work system to positions of responsibility in *my* office. Not surprisingly, in view of the slipshod nature of his work, young Scullion had not showed up to face the music this morning, and I was forced to send for Miss Brady and ask her to fetch him, or a medical certificate to account for his absence.

Miss Brady refused to go!!!

It appears that young Scullion lives in the vicinity of the Shankill Road, and Miss Brady states that her father has forbidden her to be seen in what she terms 'Prod-Land'.

I had not realized that Miss Brady was an R.C. I am very surprised that Mr Blaney engaged her in the circumstances. However, in the light of the disgraceful looting and hooliganism in the Shankill Road on the Sabbath Day (A day devoted by all *true* Protestant Loyalists to the study of the scripture, and not to looting and burning and assaults upon our police, and the pilfering of goods from decent traders), in the light of the desecration of the Lord's Day by vandals and hooligans on the Shankill (However much they may have been provoked by the vile attack by R.C.s on the Junior Orange Parade on Saturday) I suppose that a visit by

Miss Brady (albeit as an agent of Blaney, Aiken and McMaster, acting upon my instructions) might be seen as an act of R.C. provocation. Now I come to think of it, she does *look* very Papish indeed.

I shall have to arrange for someone else to be placed in charge of the petty cash.

The events of Saturday (When R.C.s from the ill named Unity Walk block of flats attacked an innocent inter-denominational parade of Young Orangemen) and the Lord's Day when bands of young hooligans and tearaways riled by the persistent provocation of R.C.s and the Socialists, Anarchists and Trotskyite Communists of Queen's University (What a misnomer!! I should call it Traitor Hall!!! These young Moscow spawn should have their grants cut off and their behinds soundly *belaboured* ... surely a fitting *end* for Socialists!!!) looted and terrorized the innocent Loyalists and old age pensioners of the Shankill and Crumlin Roads, have played into the hands of Ulster's enemies and done great damage to the commerce of Our Little Bit of Britain. How can our Minister of Commerce face the outside world and hope to continue to attract outside interests? Loyalists everywhere, and particularly in the areas where these Young Yah-Boos broke loose, must deplore the dreadful events of the week-end, and particularly the foul misuse of the Lord's Day. It is particularly distressing that the Royal Ulster Constabulary (who until this time had acted fairly and impartially, even withstanding the attacks of terrorists and Republicans at Burntollet Bridge and in Londonderry) should have seen fit to use riot shields and batons against Loyalists in the heart of a Loyalist area. One must wholly concur with the statement of the Shankill Defence Association who say (and I quote direct from this morning's *Newsletter* which, I am happy to record, gives due prominence to the story):

'It is our belief, however, that the rioting was the direct result of police provocation and unimaginable brutality to defenceless women and children ... ... We demand that the same action be taken against armed Republicans as has been taken against women and children, whose only crime was loyalty. We make it clear that the police are no longer the friends of Ulster Loyalists and never can expect our help again.'

Things have come to a pretty pass when Loyal Protestants can be assaulted in their own Province by Our Side, while R.C. Hooligans and Republicans go free to do as they please.

I said as much to Mr Blaney, when he called in to speak about the affairs of the outer office (Of which I have recently been appointed Under-Manager. Mr Blaney is himself Manager of the Outer Office, and, as he is a partner, I am, in effect, in charge). I am sorry to say that Mr Blaney did *not* agree with my analysis of the situation.

'Harland,' he said. 'Shops and stores have been looted. Hundreds of thousands of pounds of damages have been sustained. According to this morning's paper, at least 200 people have been injured in street fighting. These events took place in the heart of a Protestant area. Protestant premises looted by Protestants. A Protestant policeman assaulted by Protestants and set on fire. I, for one, cannot see that the police could have behaved in any other manner.'

'Ah, but Mr Blaney,' I said, patiently. 'What about the R.C.s?'

'Well, what about them?' he said.

'What I want to know, Mr Blaney,' I said, 'is why the police did not baton the R.C.s as they batoned Loyalist grandmothers and babes in arms?'

'Your so called Loyalist grandmothers were looting

for drink, Harland,' he said. 'No doubt they brought their grandchildren with them.'

'And what about the R.C.s in Bogside?' I said.

Then Mr Blaney said the most extraordinary thing. 'As I understand it Harland,' he said, 'your precious R.U.C. beat the bejasus out of the people of Bogside, on a number of occasions. Any trouble they get up there is only what they've asked for.' And with that he slammed down the figures on my desk and stalked out.

I have worked for Blaney, Aiken and McMaster for many years, man and boy. They have always been good workmasters, a fine Protestant Firm in the old tradition, and yet I may say that following this degrading outburst of young Mr Blaney's I came closer than I have ever been in my life before to handing in my notice on the spot. I wonder what old Mr Blaney would say? However, I thought of Victoria Alberta and the children (and Mother) and held my peace. I have never before discussed politics with young Mr Blaney, and now I shall forever hold my peace (Unless, of course, he sees fit to apologize to me). Even so it escapes my understanding that a man of Mr Blaney's background and education ... his Father was a Grand Master of the Orange Lodge ... could have been so misled by R.C. propaganda.

It seems to make no difference to him that these rioters and students in Derry and on their unruly march at Burntollet were openly provoking the Protestant people and threatening to proclaim a Trotskyite R.C. Republic, and that our police had to control them and acted with admirable restraint ... whereas this latest example of brutality to innocent Loyalists, O.A.P.s and babes in arms on the Shankill is a clear example of discrimination. Although an open and avowed follower of Captain O'Neill I must now admit myself to have been in error. The Rev. Paisley is quite right. Our Protestant Constitution is being undermined. It is up to all of us moderates to stand up and be counted. No Surrender!!!!

On the way home this evening I called in at Mr Bingham's shop to collect the *Belfast Telegraph* and told him, in confidence, about my interview with young Mr Blaney.

'I shall put him on my list,' said Mr Bingham.

'What list?' I said.

'Never you mind,' said Mr Bingham. 'A wink is as good as a nod to an honest man.'

I confess that I cannot quite see what he was talking about.

I am glad to see that our Prime Minister, Major Chichester-Clark, has now returned from his well earned holiday in Switzerland and taken over the helm. Funny that we should both take up our duties once more on the same day. I am sure we can rely on the Major to take a firm stand.

Perhaps the police would not have acted so hastily against Loyalists if he had been in the chair.

Mr Bingham pointed out an interesting item in to-day's paper to me. A Mr Arthur Bottomley, Labour M.P. for Middlesborough East and a former Commonwealth Secretary, has been shooting his mouth off!!! He suggests that the Pope and the Archbishop of Canterbury should visit Ulster together.

'I'd like to get my boot at his Bottomley!!' I said, brilliantly, considering that it was quite off the cuff.

'If the Pope sets foot in Ulster,' said Mr Bingham, 'we'll stuff the pill up his arse!'

'What I want to know,' I said, 'is why the Pope doesn't acknowledge the Constitution of Ulster. After all, we are a Moderate people. We have nothing against R.C.s here, have we?'

'Not if they know their place,' said Bingham.

'Like the Blackies,' I said.

'Some Blackies are Protestants,' said Mr Bingham.

'Most Blackies are R.C.s,' I said. 'I know. My son Craig has to deal with them. You can tell they're R.C.s from the way they behave.'

'Not that I've got anything against Blackies or R.C.s,' said Bingham. 'Not if they behave themselves.'

'After all,' I said. 'You sell the *Irish News*, don't you? That's an R.C. paper. But you don't discriminate against it.'

'No indeed,' said Bingham. 'Business is business. They have as much right to their newspaper as we have. We don't have any censorship here, not like their Republic.'

'Mind you,' I said, 'they must have something there. A little bit of censorship would do no harm, if it got rid of muck like that little book you showed me.' Then I showed him my letter. Bingham agreed that it was a responsible and public spirited document. We looked through the *Belfast Telegraph* letter page, but it had not been included. I think, and Bingham agrees, that we should form an Ulster Decencies League to challenge Communistic muck-purveyors in public and put them to shame. Bingham has handed over to me some other booklets of the same nature for inspection, and has promised to obtain more from his supplier. With this material we shall have a sound basis of evidence upon which to rest our case.

'About the *Irish News*,' Bingham said, as I was going. 'You needn't think that because I stock it, I agree with what it says.'

'Of course not, Bingham,' I said.

'As a matter of fact,' he said, 'I make a careful note of the people who buy it, just in case.'

'In case what?' I said.

'In case it might come in handy,' he said, mysteriously.

I sometimes think that there may be more to Bingham than is at first apparent.

I got home to find Mother installed in the front room, and Victoria Alberta upstairs in her bed. She says she will not come down until Mother leaves the sitting-room.

I have told Victoria Alberta, quite firmly, that she must welcome my Mother into the Home as she would her own. Fortunately her own is dead.

'Where have you been?' Mother said, when I came in with her tea on a tray.

'Working, Mother,' I said.

'Aha,' she said, wagging her finger at me. 'I know.'

She would not tell me what she knew, despite persistent questioning on my part. Also she says that she is not partial to sardines on toast, and will not eat them. I responded that this was no reason to allow an extra large sardine to fall on Victoria Alberta's fire-mat, and Mother, I am happy to say, had the good grace to apologize for dropping it. Unfortunately the sardine somehow became attached to the sole of Mother's shoe; however, it matches the carpet.

The photographs in tonight's *Belfast Telegraph* are most depressing. Policemen with riot shields ... and Our Flag on a barricade. Two pages of photographs, and the headline:

'SUNDAY ON THE SHANKILL ROAD AS MOB
TERROR REIGNS SUPREME'

I must say that I do not think they should refer to Loyalists defending their homes from the R.C.s as a mob. I expect that most of the looting was done by R.C.s who infiltrated the Protestant area. It is like the Blackies in Britain. They go into an area and cause trouble and innocent people whose only concern is the upkeep of the homes they fought for in the two world wars are blamed. There are, I know, some Blackies at Queen's University (Traitor Hall) and I shouldn't be at all surprised if they were mixed up in the Revolutionary People's Democracy run by Michael Farrell

(Michael Gun-Barrel, I call him) and that fellow Boyle who tried to infiltrate the Unionist Party. He put it about that he was going to be one of Our candidates, but I am glad to say that honest men soon sent him packing.

How can Catholics be in the Unionist Party when they won't recognize Our Constitution? I see that Boyle has now joined the English Conservatives. I expect they will see through him and send him packing. My son Craig is quite right when he says that we must keep a firm hand on these students and revolutionaries, not to mention the Blackies. He says he knows Blackies who earn more than he does, and Craig is fully qualified (Although not thought good enough by our authorities to attend Queen's University ... no doubt because he could not subscribe to their Civil Rights (Uncivil Rioters) doctrines).

I see that an ex-independent M.P. for Queen's University is learning to speak Irish. It all adds up. The only people who speak Irish are the R.C.s and it is therefore clear that she wishes to mix with R.C.s and ignore the Protestant majority. Well, we, the majority, speak *British*, and I shall write and tell her so!!

As Victoria Alberta is still in a highly nervous state I have taken it upon myself to conceal today's newspapers from her, as I am sure she would be most upset by the course events have taken. Perhaps it is just as well that Mother sat upon the Television set, as otherwise all this unpleasantness would have been brought right into our living-room.

I think I shall paint the spare room blue, to cheer myself up. Then perhaps I will be able to persuade Victoria Alberta to allow Mother to occupy it.

Victoria Alberta tells me that No. 10 Boyne Villas, the house next door to ours, has been sold to a young couple. She spoke to the woman over the fence and was quite impressed. She says they seem to be our sort of person.

Someone has left a can of methylated spirit in the outside loo. I stubbed my foot upon it while searching for the coal shovel, and have had to apply a plaster.

I must speak to Victoria Alberta once more about unnecessary domestic purchases.

TUESDAY, FIFTH OF AUGUST

A wonderfully happy day for all at Boyne Villas. This morning, during breakfast, we received a telephone call from our daughter Angelica Elizabeth.

She is coming home!!

Truly Boyne Villas runneth over with joy!!!

I need scarcely say that her return to the fold will be the occasion for a little informal family celebration, although the precise nature of this has not yet been decided. Mother, upon being acquainted with the happy news, suggested that we have what she termed a 'booze up', but I hardly think that this would be suitable, and Victoria Alberta agrees with me. However, more of that anon. Angelica Elizabeth is to arrive by the late aeroplane tonight, and I have arranged with Victoria Alberta that we shall travel up to the airport to greet our daughter together.

What a happy day!!!

The only shadow cast upon the happy hour was a curious exchange with my wife, Victoria Alberta, before I left home this morning. She began by asking Mother to leave us, which Mother (quite rightly in my opinion) refused to do. Mother is an elderly person, and has some difficulty in getting about, and I think that Victoria Alberta sometimes fails to make allowances for this.

'Very well,' said Victoria Alberta. 'Please sit down Augustus, and I shall say what I feel I must say to you.'

'Say on, my dear,' I said, in such a jovial mood that even her air of obvious concern could not prick the bubble of my elation.

'Augustus,' said Victoria Alberta, standing pensively by the table (From which I regret to say she had not yet cleared the breakfast things, although we had finished our provender some time before). 'I have been a good wife to you, have I not?'

'Victoria Alberta,' I said. 'I am not a man for fancy phrases (indeed I am not) but if there were a poll held tomorrow to name Ulster's Top of the Mums, I should, without hesitation, vote for you.'

'Please be serious, Augustus,' she said.

'My dear,' I said, 'I shall try. But this is such a joyous day, so light is my heart that...'

I am sorry to say that at this point Victoria Alberta interrupted me, a little more sharply than is customary between us. I believe that a married couple should be more polite to each other than to outsiders, not less, and that the moral strength inherent in the traditional courtesies gives fibre to a marriage. However, as my wife was obviously in a highly nervous state, I accepted her apologies, and sat back waiting for her to proceed with what she had to say, though with half an eye to the clock, which was fast moving on.

'Augustus,' she said. 'Elizabeth is coming home...'

'Angelica Elizabeth,' I put in, for I can see no point in bestowing a beautiful name upon a child and then resorting to diminutives.

'Angelica Elizabeth is coming home,' she said. 'The child has thrown herself upon us ... no, no, please let me continue, Augustus. (As I would have interrupted her). The child has shown true generosity of spirit in stepping down from the stand she had taken...'

'An unreasonable stand,' I pointed out.

'That is a matter of opinion,' said Victoria Alberta, getting quite worked up. 'Whatever you may think, Elizabeth has swallowed her pride and is making a considerable sacrifice to come home. Why, on her present salary at St Matthew's, the fare alone must represent a substantial financial loss ... you should appreciate that, if nothing else.'

'Indeed I do,' I said. 'These air fares are a disgrace, and the deliberate result of the Labour Government's dislike of our elected Government at Stormont.'

'The child is coming home,' said Victoria Alberta, 'and she must be made to feel she is at home.'

'As she will be,' I said.

'In that case, Augustus,' said Victoria Alberta. 'I must ask you to avoid contradicting the child in every single word she says.'

There was a terrible silence.

'You've got more sense than I thought you had, 'Bertie,' said my Mother from the corner.

'Thank you, Mother,' said Victoria Alberta.

I was quite astounded. No, that is an understatement. I was truly flabbergasted. However, time was pressing on and, as Victoria Alberta's request was so obviously based on her current highly emotional state, I did not trouble to have words with her, but simply said that I would do my best to be an agreeable and loving Daddy, as indeed I have been, at all times.

'Like Father, like son,' said Mother.

'This time, *I* thank you, Mother,' I said. 'My Father was a wonderful man. I am proud to be compared to him.'

'Dirty old bastard,' said Mother.

At this point Victoria Alberta left the room.

I reprimanded Mother, but I fear that my words had little effect. I then went in search of Victoria Alberta, but found that she had locked herself in the spare room. I knocked several times, but she refused to admit me, nor would she speak a word. However, I said my say.

'I have always done my best to be a good daddy,' I said, 'and I hope that I shall continue to do so. I am sure you will agree that, in the case of Craig, my labours have borne fruit as witness his excellent academic record and fine character. I am truly proud of my son. If our daughter and I have not seen eye to eye upon all matters, it has been through no fault of my own. Indeed I should say I have bent over backwards to understand the whims of that young madam.'

No word came from behind the locked door.

With that I went back down the stairs, meeting Mother on the way.

'I have told Victoria Alberta where I stand, Mother,' I said. 'And I will thank you not to interfere further in matters which do not concern you.'

'If 'Bertie doesn't come out of the bogs soon,' said Mother, 'I shall shit myself.'

'Victoria Alberta is in her room,' I said, coldly, and passed on my way. I shall have to do something about Mother's language.

As I reached the foot of the stairs I caught the unmistakeable sound of a lavatory cistern flushing, so I fear that all my good words had been spent on thin air.

My interview with Victoria Alberta and Mother upset me, and there is no point in maintaining that it did not. I arrived at Bingham's shop to collect my newspaper in a most perturbed frame of mind, which wasn't helped at all by the news that street fighting has continued in our city. I am now convinced that reports that Protestants had been attacked by our R.U.C. men must have been the result of a series of misunderstandings. Possibly our police mistook Loyalists for Republican interlopers. Certainly it would seem that a handful of Loyalists acted in an unprincipled manner, and no doubt many of the others turned out in an attempt to protect the good name of Ulster from their activities. The police arriving late on the scene, no doubt mistook these good men for rioters. Last night, it appears, our police were caught between rival mobs in the riot areas, and petrol bombs were lobbed at them. However the 'B' Specials have now moved into the Protestant area, and I am sure that we can trust them to look after Ulster's image, even if some Loyalists still have grounds to doubt the full time R.U.C. Also the Orange Lodges have arranged for their members to patrol the streets and prevent looting. All very sound.

Bingham pointed out to me a most significant paragraph, a statement by the Rev. Ian Paisley calling for the greatest possible Loyalist Parade in Newry on the 16th of this month. This is what the Rev. Paisley had to say:

> 'It is the abysmal failure of our government that has led to this situation developing in the province ... we are now reaping the dreadful harvest of O'Neillism.'

'Well,' Bingham said. 'What do you think of that Harland? Still Backing O'Neill?'

I had to admit that he was right. The Captain did betray us, straight into the hands of the Republicans. Thank God for the strong men of Ulster, who were not afraid to speak out.

Bingham also pointed out to me that the M.P. Bottomley, who proposed that the Pope (of all people) should visit N. Ireland, is a founder member of our so-called Labour Party. Which only goes to show, doesn't it? I expect he is acting for Harold Wilson, trying to undermine Our Constitution. We all know Harold would like to wash his hands of Ulster, oh yes. Ulster has returned Conservatives and Unionists to Westminster for years, and always will ... that's why Wilson wants to give us to the Republic.

Mr Paisley's parade will show them where Ulster's heart is. Newry may be an R.C. town, but it belongs to us, and we intend to make it very plain to them.

Let them slip off over the border to their R.C. Republic if they don't like Loyalist Parades.

The morning at the office was marked by the return of young Scullion to his duties, complete with a spectacular bandage, covering one eye and the crown of his head. As he had failed to notify the firm of his intention to be absent on Monday, I had a little interview with him in the Stationery Stockroom, which I use as an impromptu office on such occasions. I think it would be only right and proper if the firm allocated me, as official under manager of the Outer Office, a room of my own; however, owing to pressure of space, I have to make do with a desk (Quite the largest in the whole establishment, and always overflowing with work) and make use of the Stationery Stockroom when I have occasion to reprimand my staff.

It is Scullion's misfortune to have what I would call a furtive face. The lad cannot help looking as though he is in the wrong (Which he often is).

'Please sir,' he said. 'I was bashin' R.C.s.'

'On the Sabbath, Scullion?' I said, gravely.

'Please sir, they were bashin' us, and we were bashin' them.'

'You have yet to answer my question, Scullion,' I said. 'Were you, or were you not, engaging in riotous behaviour on the Lord's Day?'

He hung his head.

'You are aware, Scullion, that it was most improper of you not to notify the firm of your intention to be absent?'

'Please sir, I was in hospital. Me head's split from one ear to the other.'

'That is unfortunate, Scullion, but no concern of mine, or of Blaney, Aiken and McMaster who, I must remind you, pay for your daily bread.'

Scullion had the grace to look abashed. Although he is not my favourite person, and was manifestly unsuitable to be entrusted with the monthly figures during my absence on holiday (and against my precise instructions) I could not but help feel a pang for the lad.

'Tell me, Scullion,' I said. 'How did the battle fare?'

'We was all over the Fenians,' he said, with graphic simplicity.

'And your wounds?'

'I'm a Prod, sir. That's what being a Prod is, isn't it? Skinning Teagues.'

Silently, I took his hand. The boy seemed quite nonplussed. 'Do not be abashed, Scullion,' I said, 'I too am a Protestant, and should the hour of battle come, I too will stand shoulder to shoulder with you.'

'Were you up the Shankill Sunday, sir?' he said.

'Sunday,' I said, 'is the Lord's Day.'

'That doesn't stop the R.C.s sir.'

'The R.C.s are not Christians, Scullion,' I said. 'We should set an example to them. I am sure the Lord Jesus Christ would not have us fight on His Father's Day. Six days shalt thou labour, Scullion. Six days ought to be enough to see the R.C.s off, with God on our side.'

'That's right, sir,' said Scullion.

'Well Scullion,' I said, 'try to do better next time. And please remember to notify the firm if you intend to be absent in future.'

'Please sir, I was unconscious.'

'No doubt,' I said. Then, for the lad's own good, I remembered to warn him not to mention his reason for absence to Mr Blaney the younger, who is evidently not in sympathy with Loyalists.

'He's not a Teague, is he sir?' said Scullion, meaning a Roman Catholic.

'This is a Protestant firm, Scullion,' I said. 'The Young Mr Blaney was brought up a good Christian like the rest of us. What faith ... if any ... he professes now, I could not say.'

Scullion looked perplexed, as well he might.

'Be that as it may, Scullion,' I said. 'However misguided Mr Blaney may be in his political beliefs outside office hours, our duty is to serve him and the firm, within them. He is our superior, Scullion, just as I am your superior and you are the superior of ... say ... Miss Brady. If our positions were reversed, then one might take a different view of things. If for instance, the views expressed by Mr Blaney were to be expressed by someone in a lowly position, someone from whom one could expect subservience, one might adopt a more positive approach. Do you follow me, Scullion?'

'No sir,' he said. He really is not a very intelligent chap, although his heart is in the right place.

'In that case, Scullion,' I said. 'You may go. But do remember to knock when you enter the typists' room ... you might disturb Miss Brady whilst she is telling her beads.'

'Do you mean ...'

'Yes, Scullion, I do.'

I fancy that life will not be so comfortable for Miss Brady from now on. No doubt she has some private and personal arrangement with Mr Blaney (I cannot believe that he would otherwise have engaged her) but I fancy that she may soon wish to change her job.

On arriving home I was surprised to see the young man in the black leather jacket who was so discourteous to myself and Bingham walking past my house. I can only say that it came as an even greater shock when he turned into No. 10 and opened the door with a latchkey.

I had not expected to have a person of that character as my next door neighbour. If his reading matter ... the *Irish News* and the *Morning Star* (A communist newspaper) ... is anything to go by, we may all find ourselves blown up in our beds.

I mentioned this to Victoria Alberta, but she seemed

quite distracted by the imminent arrival of our daughter, Angelica Elizabeth, and would only confirm that the young man was in fact alike in description to the person she had seen the previous day.

I nipped across to tell William Fullerton the bad news, but he had not yet returned from work. His wife informs me that William has recently enrolled in the Special Constabulary, and is very taken up with their affairs. She seems to consider (or I deemed by her manner that she thought so) that I should take similar steps. However I went out of my way to mention my duty in the A.R.P. during the war, and the damage to my ear drum. I left her polishing the rifle with which William had been issued. She was a little too proud of it for my taste.

Mother and Victoria Alberta have had a heart to heart talk, and I hope that matters between them will now settle into the harmony one has a right to expect in one's home. It appears that the methylated spirit in the outside 'loo was purchased for Mother, who uses it to bathe her feet in.

I am happy to say that my letter has appeared in this evening's *Belfast Telegraph*. Bingham congratulated me upon it when I picked up my paper, and I am sure that others will not be slow to follow suit. At the same time Bingham gave me three more magazines which he had procured for eventual submission to the Ulster Decencies League when we have formed it. They are *Nylon*, *Lash* and *Puss*. Bingham insists that I should pay for these in order to keep his books straight, and I have done so in the expectation of a refund from the Committee (when formed). Otherwise Bingham says he will agree to handle them on an exchange basis, one for two.

The rest of the evening spent in preparing for the arrival of my daughter Angelica Elizabeth. Without doubt, the Big Event of the Week.

WEDNESDAY, SIXTH OF AUGUST

My daughter Angelica Elizabeth, has come home.

Naturally we are delighted to have her back with us once more. If only Craig could be here to witness our joyous reunion. No doubt his duties in the pet cemetery and the responsibilities he has taken on with regard to keeping the Blackies in their place have prohibited him from corresponding with us recently, though I hope to hear from him shortly. At a time when our homeland has been the scene of such strife and disorder I am sure he would consider it his filial duty to correspond with his parent and mentor.

I have brought all my family up to do their duty at all times.

Unfortunately I have not yet been able to have a long conversation with my daughter to clear up our little difference. I have decided to tell her that her Mummy Victoria and I have decided to wipe the slate clean. Whatever wrongs she may have done us in the past (I shall say) however badly and inconsiderately she may have treated us, we are now prepared to open our hearts to her once more, and clasp her to the bosom of our Home. I had prepared this little homily to recite to her upon our return to Boyne Villas from the airport, but I am afraid that my daughter expressed herself as being extremely tired by the journey, and I was prevailed upon by Victoria Alberta to allow her to go straight to bed. I suppose the journey must have been tiring, (I believe the Labour Government now puts old and obsolete aeroplanes upon the Ulster route in order to discourage businessmen from coming to

Ulster) but I still believe that it would have been proper to have my say there and then. However Victoria Alberta disagreed, and, as Mother also sided with her, I stood down and agreed that our daughter should go upstairs to bed. I will not say that I had words with the two women in my life when my daughter had gone, but certainly there was a certain coldness between us, which was not aided by Mother's unfortunate comment that I was a 'dry old grease-bag, like my Father'. I told her, somewhat sharply, that she had not had so much to say while Dear Father was alive, upon which she rose to her feet, yelled that my dear Father had made her life a misery, and that she was sorry she had put up with him. She then placed her feet in the bowl of methylated spirit, and would say no more. Having told her sharply to wash out her mouth with soap, I left the room.

I may say that the final act of this farcical business was that while I, the breadwinner, retired to my bed, my wife and Mother, supposedly expressing concern about my daughter's weariness, went to her room and remained there talking for several hours, during which time my wife several times went downstairs to the kitchen and made pots of tea. Glad as I am to see Mother and Victoria Alberta striking up a working arrangement of their differences, I was forced finally to go out on to the landing to remonstrate with them, pointing out that I, at least, had a living to earn, and needed my sleep, undisturbed by idle female chatter.

I am sorry to say that this rebuke had no effect. Neither was I able to discover what it was that they were discussing so earnestly, although I managed to pass the door of the spare room several times on the pretext of nature calling.

I have resolved to speak to my wife about this matter at a later date. There should be no secrets between us. We are, and always have been, a happily united pair.

My daughter is looking well in the circumstances, although a little pale. I should say that she has also put on a little weight, although of course these things are difficult for a mere male to gauge. Certainly she does not appear as fairy light on her feet as once she was.

Met William Fullerton at the gate. He was on his way home after patrolling all night on the Shankill Road. By William's account the night passed peaceably, although he says that things still seemed tense in the riot area. Members of the Orange and Black Institutions assisted the police. William was carrying his rifle. I asked him if he had seen our new neighbour.

'What new neighbour?' William said.

'Next door,' I said. 'A most unpleasant student type of person, in a black leather jacket.'

'What's wrong with him?' asked William, yawning. (Which I do *not* think he should be allowed to do in uniform, if he is not prepared to put his hand over his mouth.)

'You are the Special Policeman, William,' I said. 'It is for you to see these things and understand. After all, that is what you are paid for. You, William, are here to protect me and other Loyalists from R.C. thugs and Republican agitators.'

'What's all this got to do with our neighbour?' William asked.

'No names, no pack drill, William,' I said. 'But you should have a little word on the Q.T. with our friend Bingham. I have reason to believe that Mr Bingham might be able to tell you a thing or two about the subversive elements in our community.'

'Bingham is as Protestant as you and I,' said William, who is slow on the uptake.

'I am not implying that Bingham is a subversive,' I said. 'Simply that he has made it his business to keep an eye on things ... doing your job for you, if I may say so William. Bingham doesn't need a uniform and a highly polished rifle to show where *his* heart lies.'

'Yes,' said William, 'I know. But now, if you'll excuse me Harland, I must get to my bed.'

And he left me quite abruptly at the gate, without so much as thanking me for my tip off.

There was no sign of the man at No. 10 when I went past his house to get my car (which I park in the concrete space in front of the Boot Repair shop) and his curtains were still drawn. I shall make it my business to find out about him. He looks like a student to me, and yet he has enough money to go buying houses in good residential districts like Boyne Villas which, although it is not the Malone Road, is exclusive in its own fashion. We are of course (At least we have always been in the past) a Loyalist Row, and indeed the display of flags and pictures of King Billy on the twelfth makes a very pretty sight, and one which has not escaped comment from the head of our local Lodge, who complimented Mr Rice at No. 3 on the red, white and blue facing he had given his garden fence. Our display on the twelfth, with bunting, flags, and the touching up of the wall painting on the gable at the end of the row, is well worthy of Good King William and would, I am sure, delight the heart of any visiting Loyalist who happened to pass down our street on his way to somewhere else. By the by, it is an interesting fact, and one upon which I have often commented to Mr Douglas at No. 23, (who is responsible for the overall decoration of our street), that the houses in the better off parts of town, Malone and Balmoral, where so many of our prominent Unionist citizens live, are by no means as forthcoming with their expressions of Loyalist Opinion as we, the more humble people of Belfast, would hold ourselves to be. I suppose that the streets up there are too wide for bunting, and of course the distance between houses set in their own grounds tends to militate against the spirit of Loyal good fellowship from which our own street decorations spring. It still seems to me that they, with all their riches, might rise to at least a Loyal arch on the Malone Road, to match those in practically every little street inhabited by the workers.

There is, of course, one law for the rich and another for the poor.

Of course, if these Republicans and revolutionaries would stop interfering with the economic development of Ulster we should all be rich, Protestant and Catholic alike, living in harmony as good neighbours. As Captain O'Neill has said, there is really nothing to stop Roman Catholics living like good Protestants. I am sure that he was right, but blind prejudice and Republicanism on the Other Side was his undoing. The Captain, however misguided, certainly did his best for us as an officer and a gentleman, and I am glad to say that Major James Chichester-Clark, our present Prime Minister, is carrying out the office in the same forthright God-fearing tradition, showing fear or favour to no man, and administrating for all, without thought for class or creed. As an ex-A.R.P. man myself, I find it interesting to note how many members of our Cabinet are also ex-officers in H.M. Forces. It adds to one's sense of belonging.

Mr Bingham is most upset by the goings on in Lisburn. It is terrible that, at times of crisis like this, Loyalists should be subjected to the undermining of the faith for which we stand by those within our own ranks.

He practically thrust the *Newsletter* at me, when I went into the shop.

'Have you seen this, Harland!' he exclaimed, pointing to a heading on the front page.

There it was, in black and white. 'Sunday Swings Row: Police Called.'

I took the paper from him and read the piece in shocked silence.

It would appear that Republican and Communistic agitators have taken over the Lisburn Borough Council, and have passed a resolution recommending that the playground swings in that town should be opened to the public upon the Sabbath Day. I am glad to say that this Godless decision was not allowed to pass without comment, for a number of Loyalist members of the Rev. Ian Paisley's Ulster Constitution Defence Committee managed to gain admittance to the council chamber and made their views known to the council from the public gallery, quoting the Scriptures. (Which are quite explicit on the subject. Six Days Shalt Thou Labour.) Of course the *Newsletter* dare not say that it is Communists and Republicans, but goodness knows it is plain enough. It appears from their report that the swings are to be opened as the result of a deputation from the South Antrim Labour Party (Who obviously have a vested interest in bringing about the downfall of our Protestant majority, as it affects twelve seats in the Westminster Parliament which their Harold would dearly like to be rid of). With the activities of the local Labour parties and the Labour Lawyers, together with outright discrimination against the Unionist administration by the Westminster Government, it is obvious that the British Labour Movement is by now taking its orders from known Communists and Republicans in Dublin, whose aim is a Communist state ruled over by the Pope. One Pope/No Vote should be their slogan.

At least one honest Ulster Councillor remains in Lisburn however, and I quote from the *Newsletter* report: 'Councillor Shanks said it was only the thin end of the wedge, and the council was paving the way for the opening of the new swimming pool on Sundays.' No doubt he is quite right. It is regrettable that the R.U.C. allowed themselves to be used as the tool of these red thugs at Lisburn, and cleared the public gallery of Loyalists. A Councillor M'Keown (probably an R.C.) went so far as to suggest that Loyalists who objected to children swinging on Sunday did not object to their fathers drinking in two clubs in town ... a typical slur.

Bingham has put Councillor M'Keown on his list.

Bingham had a serious word to say to me on the current situation. He took me into the back of his shop and showed me a collection of staves and solid looking sticks.

'What do you think these are for, Harland?' he said.

'Protecting our homes, Bingham,' I said, adding that I was glad to see that one local Loyalist at least was taking the necessary steps, as our local 'B' Special, (William Fullerton) did not seem to be taking a pride in his work.

'I cannot carry all these arms myself, Harland,' he said. 'I need the aid of loyal men in the neighbourhood. Men of gumption, preferably men with previous British Military experience.'

I told him of my service in the A.R.P., and the war wound to my ear drums. (Which has still not been recognized by the authorities.)

'I will say no more for the present Harland,' said Bingham. 'But I hope you will hold yourself ready for any emergency, should one arise.'

Then we saluted each other. It was a solemn moment. I left Bingham's humble shop with something of the old A.R.P. spirit pulsing through my veins. We fought the Hun, and licked him when all seemed to be up. Ulstermen are not to be strangled with Moscow Rosary beads, indeed not.

Mr Blaney was waiting for me at the office, which was unfortunate, as owing to my interview with Bingham (Which was, I like to think, more important than mere clockwatching) I was late.

'In at last I see, Harland,' he said.

'I assure you that any time owing to the firm will be made up sir,' I said. (Since the affair of the police assault upon our Loyalists (Mistaken for Republican interlopers) I have retained a strictly business manner when conversing with my immediate superior.)

'I should like to talk to you about these figures Harland,' he said, laying the monthly figure book before me.

'I am sorry Mr Blaney,' I said. 'But those figures are no responsibility of mine.'

'You are in charge of the Outer Office, Harland,' he said. 'Any work done in that office is your responsibility.'

I retained an icy calm. 'That is normally the case sir,' I said, 'and I think I may say without fear of contradiction that you will agree that seldom if ever have you found cause to find fault with my work, or the work emanating from staff appointed by me to undertake a particular task or tasks falling within the compass of the Outer Office, where my own particular responsibility *vis-à-vis* the firm lies. I think you will agree sir, that I have never given cause for complaint in the performance of my duties.'

He interrupted me, quite brusquely. 'These figures, Harland, are manifestly incorrect.'

'I repeat sir, that those figures are not my responsibility.'

'And I repeat that you are in charge of the Outer Office, Harland,' he said.

'Not when I am on holiday sir,' I said, and when that didn't seem to have any visible effect on him, I went on. 'Not when jobs are allocated to underlings not fitted to undertake them, without my opinion being consulted.'

'You checked these figures, Harland?' he said.

'Indeed I did sir,' I said.

'And you saw them to be incorrect?'

'I did sir.'

'And you did nothing about it?'

'Those figures were compiled by young Scullion, on, he gives me to understand, your authority, and against my precise instruction. With due respect, Mr Blaney, I would not presume to correct work done under your personal instruction and supervision!'

Of course, I fairly took the wind from his sails with that!!!

'This is most unsatisfactory, Harland,' he managed to stutter, after a moment or two.

'I agree sir,' I said, magnanimously. 'And I will be glad to take the book back and see that the figures are corrected, given your authority to do so.'

'Do that, Harland,' he said, and slammed the figures down upon my desk.

'One moment, if you please, Mr Blaney sir,' I said, as he turned to leave. 'I take it that you will agree that my authority is complete in relation to the Outer Office, and not to be tampered with?'

'That is the case, Harland,' he said.

'In which case, sir,' I said, 'may I take it that I will in future be consulted on all matters reflecting upon the work of my department, particularly upon matters relating to the allocation of work?'

'Harland,' he said. 'You were on holiday. How could you possibly be consulted? You had left no instructions. The monthly figures had to be compiled, had they not?'

'My views on Scullion are well known sir,' I said. 'And as to my being on holiday: I was never, I fancy, far from the telephone. Had you wished to contact me to consult on this matter I should have made myself readily available, in the interests of the firm.'

That squashed him. Of course, no reply was possible, and he had the grace not to attempt to make one, though it is a sign of the weakness in the man that he did not own up to being in the wrong and apologize. No doubt he has his mind on his more *intimate* affairs ... I wonder if Mrs Blaney knows about our Miss Brady in the typing pool ... no doubt she would be interested to learn whom her husband takes for those little business dinners top executives are so fond of. I think, and I have often suggested it through the medium of the suggestions box, that junior executives (such as myself) should be encouraged to fraternize with the junior executives of our clients, and to lunch with them at the expense of the firm, thus cultivating good business relations. I cannot see that a little vino and a good steak could cost the firm so much, and I'm sure it would do a lot more good than Mr Blaney taking R.C. typists out to dine.

I must find out what is going on between those two. Obviously Blaney would not have engaged an R.C. unless he was getting something there. They think that so long as they can go to the Confessional Box and tell their Priest about it it doesn't matter what they do. I am told that nearly all Prostitutes are either R.C.s or Blackies, and the Jew-boys run them.

I have spoken to Scullion about his figures. He was most respectful, and promised to do better next time. Quite a change for Scullion, and a welcome sign of unity. Of course Protestants must always do their best to hold together in times of danger. Nevertheless I am glad that Scullion did not overhear my conversation with Mr Blaney as, although I stood up for my rights, he might regard what I had to say as a betrayal. When we had disposed of the matter of the figures and discussed Scullion's wounds (At some length, I fear. It appears that one of his cousins is in danger of losing the sight of one eye, having been struck by the baton of an R.C. policeman. I must say it had not occurred to me previously that Roman Catholics were allowed to join the R.U.C. (As they do not, of course, recognize our Constitution) but perhaps this infiltration accounts for the attacks made by the police upon Loyalists. I am sure that R.C. policemen would have been only too glad to mislead Protestant policemen into believing that Loyalist Grandmothers defending their homes were in fact Republican interlopers. In the event Scullion knows the name and address of the R.C. policeman who struck his cousin, and assures me that the matter will soon be put right!!!!) After, as I say, we had discussed Scullion and Scullion's cousin at some length, the conversation turned to the enemy nearer home (or work).

'Scullion,' I said, 'I am sorry to say that I have formed the opinion based upon the fact of her employment here without any of us being informed of her background, that Miss Brady and our immediate superior, Mr Blaney the younger, have formed a liaison.'

Scullion did not seem to understand me.

'I believe that our employer may be exceeding the normal bounds of an employer/employee relationship with Miss Brady,' I said.

'Stuffing her?' said Scullion, who is a vulgar tongued boy.

I told him to go and wash his mouth out with toilet soap.

'I wouldn't mind going in up her crack, sir,' Scullion said, accompanying his remark with a gesture familiar to us all from the wartime days, when Sir Winston showed Jerry the door.

'You will have to ask Mr Blaney about Miss Brady's ... er ... crack, Scullion,' I said. 'No doubt he knows the way to go about it.'

'Lovely grub,' said Scullion.

'Be that as it may, Scullion,' I said. 'I think that you and I, as Loyal Protestants and employees of Blaney,

Aiken and McMaster, have a duty both to the Partners and to *Mrs* Blaney to find out the truth. We shall point the finger at the transgressor and his Papish whore.'

'She's got big blabby tits too,' said Scullion.

'No doubt she would welcome your interest, Scullion,' I said, with distaste. It is a pity that the boy cannot be persuaded to join a decent youth club, or one of our flute bands. 'Be that as it may, our concern, our sole concern, is to ascertain the truth. To this end, I must ask you to assist me.' Then I outlined my plan to him.

In essence it is simple.

Scullion is to follow Miss Brady home in the evenings and, with the assistance of another of his cousins (This one, I understand, with *No* injuries) to keep a watch on her home and her movements during the time she is not at work. If, as I believe to be the case, she is in fact Mr Blaney's whore, the relationship should soon manifest itself, and we will then have to consider our next step.

Scullion agrees with me that it is an excellent plan, and agrees to do as I say, providing that I will meet his expenses, which he assures me will not be excessive. As I know the boy is from a very poor background I have agreed to this, provided he and his cousin exercise *their* discretion, while spending *my* money. Should I receive confirmation of my suspicions, I shall feel it my duty to make it known to the Partners, by writing the details of time and place upon a plain (unsigned) piece of paper and inserting it in the suggestions box. Mrs Blaney is another matter, as she will obviously require evidence should she decide to take proceedings against her husband, and might in that event be prepared to cover any expenses I may have incurred through employing Scullion as my 'Private Eye'.

I am, after all, only doing my duty as a Christian. If he is not 'carrying-on' with the girl why then did he engage her to work in our offices, when he must have known her to be a member of the minority group?

On my way home I stopped off at the Bon-Bon in Constitution St. and bought a small box of chocolates as a welcome home gift for my daughter Angelica Elizabeth, but I am sorry to say that, upon my return to Boyne Villas, I learned that she had gone out for the evening, thus further postponing our conversation.

The new family at No. 10 have painted their house front white, with blue wood-work ... one would hope for a little red decoration ... perhaps that is provided by the shade of the student type husband's political beliefs!!! I have still not had occasion to pass the day with the young man or his wife, but I intend to be civil, at least until we see what way the fox jumps. Of course, all students are not as misguided as those in the Revolutionary Socialist People's Democracy, some at least have heeded the warnings of men like our Major Bunting and the Rev. Paisley and seen that organization for what it undoubtedly is, a front for extreme Catholics and Marxists.

Although disappointed at the absence of my daughter, the evening was made for me by the large bundle of letters (at least thirty) which my wife Victoria Alberta deposited beside my slippers.

'Well, Augustus,' she said, 'it looks as if you've really let yourself in for it this time.'

'Indeed it does, my dear,' I said, searching through the sideboard for my paperknife (Which I eventually found to be covered with Polyfilla. It appears that my wife had loaned it to William Fullerton for purposes unspecified, and William had returned it in this condition ... not conduct I would consider worthy of a member of our Special Constabulary).

The letters, when I had at last managed to clean my paperknife, were, on the whole satisfactory. I'm afraid that one or two vulgar persons had seen fit to exercise their crude sense of humour at my expense. I had signed my letter to the press 'At the convenience of the public' indicating my simple wish to offer my services to the community. I am sorry to say that some of these illiterate louts chose to interpret my words in a different fashion, addressing their letters:

> Augustus Harland (Ex-A.R.P.)
> The Public Lavatory,
> Boyne Villas,
> Belfast.

At least one of these communications had no stamp upon it, and my wife Victoria Alberta had to meet the expense of delivery from her housekeeping ... a matter which we shall have to adjust in the weekly book-keeping session which it is our custom to undertake on Friday nights after the television news ... although now that Mother has sat upon the set we may alter this timing.

'What do you mean, settle it?' said Mother, from her corner. 'Give her the money.'

'Please do not interfere, Mother,' I said, coldly.

'His Father was just the same, Vicky,' said Mother, addressing my wife. 'They used to say old Cunningham Harland would fight his grannie under the bed for a threepenny bit.'

My wife had the ill manners to laugh.

I stood up. 'I see,' I said, 'that there is some form of conspiracy against me in this house.'

'Not at all, Augustus,' said my wife. 'Your Mother and I have just been getting to know each other better, that is all.'

'Of that I am glad,' I said, maintaining my dignity. 'But I fancy a little respect for the Master of the House would not come amiss.'

There was a pause.

'Hark to droopy drawers,' said Mother, and started to giggle.

'And respect for the Mistress,' said my wife, and they both left me and went into the front room, where I could hear them laughing.

I must say I object to being the odd man out in my own household. I have never before known Victoria Alberta to dare to answer back to me. I fear that Mother has not been a good influence with her. I seem to remember similar incidents with the servants answering back in my Father's day, and how Mother often openly provoked them to ridicule that fine man.

Returning to the subject of letters to newspapers (With which I have had some success over the years in securing publication, both under my own name and Victoria Alberta's); an interesting epistle appeared in this morning's *Newsletter*, which I quote here in full as I think that, coupled with the disgraceful affair of the Lisburn Sunday Swings, it is significant. The letter was headed 'Fish on Fridays' and ran as follows:

Sir,

I would like to point out to the Ulster Tourist Board that recently I was stopping in a hotel in Portrush and on Friday everyone was given fish, whether they liked it or not.

They talk about Civil Rights for Roman Catholics. What about Civil Rights for Protestants in Ulster, and let others have their choice?

       Yours, etc,
       J.B.

Belfast 14.

I regard this as a serious matter, and agree fully with J.B. No wonder some Protestant youths are driven to extremist acts when the R.C.s and Civil Riotsers are allowed to get away with this sort of blatant discrimination. Is it any wonder we have riots?

Mr Balderwood of Lower Basin Street, the Hon. Sec. of U.M.P.I.R.E. (of which I am a founder member) has summoned us to a meeting on Friday of this week (8th August) to discuss the current situation in the city. I gather from him that some dramatic proposals have been put forward by the committee, and I await the meeting with interest. I shall try to inveigle Bingham into coming along, as I think an ardent activist such as he could well be useful to us, should the committee have decided (as they may well have) to take steps to protect our homes.

Ten o'clock (my bedtime) came and went, and still no sign of my daughter returning to the fold. Neither Victoria Alberta nor Mother condescended to come in to chat with me. However, I put this behind me, and went to bed with the box of chocolates I had purchased for my daughter and a copy of the magazine *Slap* which Bingham had procured for me, in pursuit of our work for the Ulster Decencies League (as yet unformed).

Most young women are not shaped at all like that, in my experience. Also there was a Blackie in it. I may say that she (the negress) was not at all physically attractive, in my opinion. I wonder what they tell the Priest in the Confessional Box after they have posed for these pictures?

At twelve o'clock, when Victoria Alberta came to bed, our daughter had still not returned home.

Upon raising the matter with Victoria Alberta, she told me that she was sure our daughter knew what it was all about.

'I hope she does *not*!' I exclaimed.

'Don't be sillier than you have to be, Augustus,' my wife said.

She clambered into bed. As I thought, her breath smelled of alcohol.

'You have been drinking, haven't you?' I said.

'If I've got to put up with your Mother,' she said, 'I'm going to make the most of it.'

'But you do not drink,' I said.

'Call it,' she said, turning her back to me and slumping down on the pillow, 'a new tactic.'

THURSDAY, SEVENTH OF AUGUST

A day of surprises, not all of them, I am sorry to say, welcome.

This morning, upon entering the bathroom to complete my morning ablutions, I was astounded to find myself confronted with a young man whom I took at first to be a burglar. I was about to take steps to raise the alarm when the thought struck me that burglars are not usually totally unclothed.

'Stand where you are,' I said, bravely. 'I am armed.'

The young man, who had not previously perceived me, turned round and stepped down from Victoria Alberta's bathroom scales, upon which he had been standing.

'Good morning, Mr Harland sir,' he said, holding out his hand with no thought for his private parts, which were quite exposed.

Thinking that he might be about to leap upon me, I promptly shut the door, and turned the key in the lock. Then I called for my wife Victoria Alberta, who came hurrying from the kitchen, frying pan in hand.

'Whatever is the matter, Augustus?' cried my wife.

'Victoria Alberta,' I snapped. 'There is a naked young man in the bathroom!'

'Yes, dear,' said Victoria Alberta. 'I expect he is washing himself.'

'I demand an explanation at once,' I said. 'Failing which I shall be forced to knock on the wall for William Fullerton.'

'Don't be silly, Augustus,' said Victoria Alberta. 'If you're in such a dreadful hurry for the bathroom why don't you use the old one at the end of the yard?'

'I wish to wash my face in my own bathroom,' I said, sternly. 'Upon opening the door, I find myself confronted by a strange young man, in a state of unashamed nudity. I have now locked that young man in, and will continue to keep him there until a reasonable excuse for his presence, naked, in my house, before breakfast, is forthcoming.'

'May I come out please, Mr Harland?' came the young man's voice, from behind the door.

'Really Augustus!' said Victoria Alberta, and she returned to the kitchen, without offering any explanation for the strange event.

'Young man,' I said, applying myself to the keyhole, 'I demand to know who you are, and what you are doing here?'

At that point my daughter appeared at the head of the stairs and, I am ashamed to say, roundly berated me in language which, at her age, I am happy to say I was not acquainted with. It appears that the naked young man in the bathroom is an acquaintance of hers, temporarily without a place to lay his head, whom my daughter had invited home for the night.

'And do you consider it was right to do so, without first requesting my permission, Angelica Elizabeth?' I said.

She had no answer to that, but retired to her bedroom. I shall also have to speak to my daughter about the length and texture of her nightshirt (if such a flimsy and insubstantial garment justifies the name. However I suppose that in the age of the mini skirt it is not to be wondered at that our young neglect the proper care of their bodies. I am sure that many of them will suffer with rheumatics in later life).

'May I come out now, please, Mr Harland?' said the young man, whom I had almost forgotten about in the hubbub. I unlocked the door and apologized to him, as a guest in my house, for my lack of courtesy, at the same time pointing out a/ that it was my house, and my permission for him to stay under my roof had not been sought, b/ that we had not been introduced and c/ that I did not consider it seemly for a young man to disrobe in a house containing females without first securing the bolt upon the door and drawing the curtains. I said that, although I was loathe to criticize any guest, particularly a guest of my daughter (And a well-spoken and polite young man I may say, which makes a change from the common muck with whom she associated while at home) I still felt it my duty as an older man to point out to him that such behaviour was unsuitable in a mixed household.

I am glad to say that the young man took it very well, showing respect for my age and authority as head of the household. He explained to me that he had merely slipped out of his robe in order to weigh himself, being under doctor's orders (as the result of a nervous complaint) to keep an eye upon his weight. He admitted his error in not securing the door before divesting himself of his clothing, and begged my pardon, which I gave him without the least hesitation.

I must say it is nice to meet a pleasant and well spoken young man these days. I certainly hope that Angelica Elizabeth will cultivate his acquaintance, as he seems to be a young man of fine character. (Though I do hope he makes a point in future of keeping his trousers on!!! (especially in the company of the opposite sex)). Mother likes him too. I heard her say to my daughter (somewhat cryptically) 'I wouldn't mind a piece of that myself, Lizzie.' I wish that Mother would learn to use the beautiful names which God (acting through the wisdom of our parents) has given us. She will call my wife 'Vicky' and my daughter 'Lizzie'. It is strange that she has never called me anything else except Augustus, though I cannot say that she always speaks the name as though she approved of it. Augustus was, of course, my Father's choice (Because of the First day of August=August 1st=my birthday).

The young man's name is the Hon. Roland Dixon, and I gather that his family is well known in Reading Berks., where his father is a man of substance. In a friendly conversation before leaving the house (I felt I should make my peace with them) he and my daughter, who had come down to breakfast together, told me of their chance meeting at the Air Terminal when Roland (He insists that I call him that instead of using his full title, a happy circumstance, as I am not altogether sure how one addresses an Honourable) chanced to be passing through on his way to Northern Ireland where he is helping the Government Information Services. I have told him that he is to regard my home as his own until such time as he finds somewhere suitable for a gentleman to reside, and I am glad to say that Roland has accepted my offer.

He is a true gentleman, with no trace of side.

Mrs Truesdale, always an objectionable woman, stopped me as I left the house today and said that she wished to complain about the revving of sports car engines in the street. Loftily, I told her that I did not possess a sports car, being quite satisfied with my Ford Anglia (a 1961 model, and quite a bargain, I fancy, at £215).

'I don't mean your old car, Mr Harland,' she said. 'I'm talking about that flashy sports car your daughter comes and goes in.'

'Ah!!' I said. 'No doubt that belongs to the Honourable Roland Dixon, my house guest. Say no more, dear lady, I shall speak to young Roland about it!' I fancy that crushed her. I left the silly woman with her mouth agape. She makes a habit of keeping the radio on loudly on Sunday mornings and, despite our repeated requests not to do so, encourages her small son Roger Henry Truesdale to play with his ball in front of Boyne Villas, thus attracting other juveniles from the neighbouring streets. It is not that we are against children, but one's own children are one thing, and the children of persons who do not even live in Boyne Villas quite another. Mr Sefton, (who lives across the road in No. 11), and I have decided that the road fronting our two houses belongs to us, dividing on the white line up the middle, and we cannot see why young Truesdale and his friends cannot play in the space in front of their own homes.

Bingham was delighted to learn that I have an employee of the Government Information Services staying with me, but he instructs me to be guarded in what I say in front of the Honourable Roland, as he understands that Mr Porter, our present Minister of Home Affairs is suspect. It is a great pity that Mr William Craig, a fine honest forthright man, was ever dismissed from that post, in which he had served Captain O'Neill's Government so well. No doubt the Captain considered that he knew best what was right for Ulster, but it seems that time is showing the truth of Mr William Craig's position. I told Bingham that I was not under the impression that the Government Information Service fell under the province of Mr Porter (Concerning whom I must make some further enquiries) and that I felt sure the Honourable Roland Dixon came of good Tory stock and would appreciate our view of the Constitutional position (Which is, I may say the view of all Loyal Moderates in Ulster. Not an inch!!!). Bingham says that we must remember the Leftist interests which are at work in England, and that young Roland may have been influenced by them. I agreed to be circumspect, while remaining sure in my own mind that the young man is solid. In any event, it should be interesting to have, as it were, an ear at the councils of the mighty. No doubt Roland will give me all the latest gen!!

Mr Blaney's car has been stolen. No doubt that accounts for his abruptness of manner in speaking to me about the schedule for next week. Unless of course, Scullion has blundered, and allowed Miss Brady to notice him.

Scullion reports that he and his cousin followed Miss Brady to her home, but saw no sign of Mr Blaney. It may well be that the losing of his car distracted him from the fleshpots!!! They report that Miss Brady lives in a very Republican area, and that her father keeps a public house. (I have always said that their movement should be known as the 'Publican Party'!!! It goes with their bottle slinging policies!!) The truth is that the licensing trade in Belfast is in the grip of subversive elements ... not surprisingly, when you consider the low type of person who will trade upon another's weakness by selling him the means of destruction ... the devil drink!! We all know that the entire economy of the Republic is based upon the firm of Guinness, which no doubt accounts for quite a lot. No doubt that noxious concern uses Holy Water for its products!! (The Church of Rome is renowned for its wine bibbing.)

I had occasion to speak to Miss Brady today about some invoices which she had mistyped. I let her see that I, for one, was not going to favour her simply because she was Teacher's Pet (Not directly of course, but by inference). Miss Brady did not bat an eyelid (Perhaps she *could* not. They were propably false!!!) No doubt she is playing *Mrs* Blaney false as well!!!

Otherwise my day at the office was uneventful, although I did have occasion to pass words with Miss Wadsworth from Accounts, who saw fit to comment favourably upon an Editorial in this morning's *Newsletter*. I will quote the piece in question *not, not*, as an example of the virtue of that newspaper, but as an example of how even fine organs of the press can be corrupted once the rot has set in. The Editorial was headed 'Victory for Sanity' and ran as follows:

'Noisy protests from inevitable last ditchers notwithstanding, the vote in favour of Sunday Swings in Lisburn was decisive, and all the more welcome for that. There is a liberalizing spirit in Northern Ireland which is stronger than those out of sympathy with it would admit.'

I must say that coupled with the main stories of the day, (That work-shy R.C. families are jumping the housing queue by making lying accusations of being threatened with violence by their fellow citizens, and attempting to use this alleged intimidation as an excuse for throwing themselves lock stock and barrel upon the public purse) *coupled* with these stories, I find this attitude of the *Newsletter* quite inexcusable. I should say that most Ulster moderate Protestants, faced with the realization that this 'liberalizing spirit' the press is so fond of means that we are to be plagued with Michael Gun-Barrel, Burn-a-debt Devil'n, John In-Hume-Ane and Ivan (The Terrible) Cooper (A renegade Protestant!!!) telling us when to say our beads and when to pass water, will cry Enough is Enough!! One Man/One Pill is a slogan *we* can understand, and otherwise they can stick their Civil Riots up their Pope. No doubt it would *not* be a tight fit!!!

Apart from that, a peaceful day at the office, and indeed a peaceful day in Belfast. Speaking to William Fullerton on the way home, he informed me that not a single petrol bomb was tossed last night, nor were any R.C. rioters and looters abroad. I am glad to say that Boyne Villas, at least, has not been visited by any of the rioting gentry, who have confined their activities to the central areas.

An excellent idea appeared in this evening's *Telegraph*; a move for peace in our community, which I intend to take up directly. It seems that a Derry nurseryman has given 225 plants to a group of young people in Derry, and it is their intention to go round the town handing these flowers out. Catholic youth will go into the Protestant areas, while Protestants will move among the Catholics (Perhaps on the Bogside they will eat the blooms!!) I think this is an excellent move. There has been some minority agitation in Derry concerning the Apprentice Boys 'Relief of Derry' Parade, a traditional day out for the whole town, in which men of all creeds draw together to celebrate the defeat of the papists by thirteen apprentices. It appears that John In-Hume-Ane and Ivan (The Terrible) Cooper have been going round causing unrest and saying that there will be street fighting in Derry if the parade takes place. Well, why should there be? The parade, an annual one, is in no way provocative, anyone can see that, and will pass off peaceably *if they will allow it to do so!* Protestants have never tampered with legal R.C. parades (Though those by the Republicans and fellow travellers of the Civil Riots and the Papal Democracy are quite another matter) and if they dare to come near us I hope the R.U.C. will give them another roasting on the Bogside. If they don't like it they can go and live in their Republic, can't they? In any event our Protestant lads are taking their lives into their hands going into the Bogside to give them flowers and the people in the Protestant areas are allowing their young people to come through unharried on the same mission, which goes to show that Protestant and Catholic can walk hand in hand behind the Union Jack and the Constitution if only these communist agitators will keep out. In any event, I think it is a good idea, and I intend to adopt it myself by taking some of Victoria Alberta's plants from the backyard and giving them to the young couple (believed to be R.C.) next door.

When I returned home it was to find my dinner in the oven, and no family. Apparently Roland had taken Mother, Victoria Alberta and my daughter for a meal in town, and they hoped I would not mind. I *do* mind, and think that I should have been considered, as I am the breadwinner, but will say no more about it for the present.

My dinner had become rather overcooked, and was not pleasant.

I paid a visit to my wife's flower pots in the backyard and removed a suitable specimen, also noting, by the by, that someone has fitted a padlock to the outside W.C. door. Most curious. I then returned to the house, polished my shoes, brushed my hair, and put on my Ulster tie (happily unstained by the ginger wine spilt on it at the time of Mother's little trouble) and went to knock on the young couple next door.

The man answered the door. 'Yes,' he said.

'Please excuse me,' I said. 'I should like to introduce myself, although I believe we have met briefly in the paper shop. My name is Augustus Harland, and I am your next door neighbour.'

'Murphy,' he said. 'Pleased to meet you.'

Murphy is generally a teague name. (R.C.)

'I don't know if you have been reading the newspapers recently, Mr Murphy,' I said, 'but it has been suggested that the interchange of simple tokens between persons of different religions might help Community relations.'

'Oh yes,' he said, and a voice from the back room, (into which I could not see as I was kept standing in the porch in a most unmannerly fashion, considering that I was almost a deputation from the neighbourhood) A voice from the back room said: 'Dermot ... your dinner's ready.'

Dermot is *almost always* an R.C. name.

'As a founder member of U.M.P.I.R.E., the Ulster Moderate Protestants Inter-Religious Educationalists group, and a leading member of the protestant community in Boyne Villas, I think it is up to me to make some little gesture to show that we Loyalists will not hold your religion against you, and wish you and your dear lady to be happy in our street.'

'That's very nice,' he said.

The voice from the background muttered something else about his dinner.

'Won't be a minute, Cathleen,' he called.

Cathleen is *often*, though not *always*, an R.C. name.

'Protestants and Catholics can live together in peace,' I said. 'I for one, as a Protestant, will not object to you being here, just so long as the place isn't overrun with your sort. This is a Protestant Country, Mr Murphy, and we are a Protestant people. A Protestant Parliament for a Protestant People is what we've got, and what we aim to hold onto.'

'So I'm told,' he said, folding his arms.

'But we like having you here,' I said. 'Perhaps when you see how very well we Protestants can run things you will begin to understand what Captain O'Neill meant when he said: "Catholics can live like good Protestants." In any event we, all of us, hope that you will.'

'Indeed,' said Mr Dermot Murphy, looking every inch of him an R.C., and probably a student. I must say I was glad to know that I had a B Special (William Fullerton) within hailing distance, and Mr Bingham at the shop ready to hand.

'Dermot,' said the voice.

'And so, Mr Murphy,' I said. 'As a token of good will between Protestants and Catholics, I should like to present you with this little potted plant. A Pot for Peace, as it were.'

'But I'm an agnostic, Mr Harland,' he said.

'Never mind about that, old chap,' I said. 'Just so long as you mind your own business, you won't keep me up at night worrying about the pictures on your walls.' Then I thrust the plant and pot into his hands, and sped away before he could so much as thank me.

I must remember to report on this little experiment to the Committee of U.M.P.I.R.E. Perhaps I should say that, although I am a founder member of U.M.P.I.R.E. I was not elected to the committee, probably because a little coterie of members (A leftist cell) got together and arranged the elections to suit their own purposes. (My son Craig had a similar experience in the White States Movement which he helped to found in California, which was infiltrated by Blackie sympathizers.) However I am happy to say that that is all that they have been able to arrange to their own satisfaction, as the ground roots members have simply ignored their more outlandish suggestions. We have, for instance, scotched their attempt to co-operate with a certain Parish Priest who wished us to join his Discussion Group and talk about Ulster Problems. Talking to them as though they were Protestants and Constitutionalists only encourages them. We were not having any of that sort of nonsense, I can tell you.

FRIDAY, EIGHTH OF AUGUST

In a confidential conversation this morning, Bingham has asked me to instruct Victoria Alberta to deliver all spare milk bottles to him for purposes of Protestant Defence. I shall do so.

It is good to see someone taking a firm line, especially after the disgraceful behaviour of our own Presbyterian Assembly. Not only did they elect to hold their meeting in Dublin, but they a/ allowed the President of the Rebel Republic to attend their deliberations and b/ stood to attention for the Rebel National Anthem.

This is not, and cannot be, right.

I for one, shall not stand back from the fray. I shall attend Dunwoody's church upon Sunday, and stand up on my hind legs to address some well chosen words to the congregation. I shall draw their attention to the recent behaviour of Rev. Dunwoody in the matter of Mother and the Gentlefolks, and to the question of the shabby behaviour of the General Assembly, as outlined above. Should my fellow churchmen not be prepared to speak out with me against the recent Romeward trend and ecumenism in our Church, I shall willingly quit their ranks. I understand that the Rev. Paisley's new church on the Ravenhill Road is a splendid edifice and I think that, in the circumstances, I should not feel ashamed to call myself a 'Free' Presbyterian ... free from all taint of Popish Republicanism.

On a happier note, I see that the R.U.C. city Commissioner, Mr Harold Wolseley, is taking a hard line with Republican and R.C. extremists who have been going around Protestant homes in R.C. areas and threatening honest householders. No doubt this has come about following attempts by R.C.s to pull the wool over the eyes of the housing authorities and jump the housing queue by claiming that Protestants and Loyalists have threatened to burn them out of their Holy Water hen hutches. It does appear that some ... a very few ... R.C.s have been threatened, but no doubt they were trouble makers and deserved it. If they don't like living in Our Protestant City they should go back to the Republic where most of them come from. They only come up here to get the family allowances and our Brew money. I am sure the Pope would welcome them back to Dublin with open arms.

It is a fact of our situation that if all the unemployed R.C.s would go back over the border where they came from there would be plenty of jobs and houses all round for Protestants. They are the *only* factor that is holding Ulster back, and yet they expect us to build our New University in Derry where they can use it, and they complain when we build our New City of Craigavon in a Unionist area instead of diverting it into the rebel counties!!! Why should we pay for them? Most of them have never done a day's work in their lives and if we had all the jobs Republican and R.C. workers have taken from good Loyalists we should have full employment. Once we get the R.C.s out it will be time enough to talk of full British Standards. At the moment they would be Damn Fool British Standards.

I am glad to say that our city has been quiet during the night.

Scullion came to me in the tea-break to report on his night's activities. He says that he has seen a number of persons in the neighbourhood who could have been

Mr Blaney, but all of them took steps to ensure that he could not get a proper glimpse of their faces.

'That is not very satisfactory, Scullion,' I said.

'I am doing my best sir,' he said.

'You have not seen anything at all, boy, have you?' I said. 'Remember that you are costing me eight shillings a night.' (Scullion had asked for eight shillings expenses. At first I told him that this was exorbitant, at which he was most upset. But he came clean and confessed that the actual expenses incurred by himself and his cousin in the course of their investigation were six shillings, but that his cousin had forced him to ask for an extra two shillings 'danger money' as they were spending a large part of the evening in a known R.C. area. I agreed to pay the extra two shillings, as this does not seem unreasonable to me, and I have every hope of getting my money back from Mrs Blaney.)

'Oh yes I have seen something sir,' he said.

'What?' I said.

'Saw her pulling off her knickers sir, through the back window.'

I may say that I reprimanded Scullion, and told him that Miss Brady, unaccompanied, pulling off her knickers, could be of no possible interest to us.

'She has a lovely arse, sir,' he said.

I think I may have made a mistake in appointing Scullion as my agent in this matter. I shall have to reconsider the whole affair, as there appears to be no evidence as yet of Mr Blaney's sordid connection with her (Due, perhaps, to the theft of his motor car, which no doubt restricts his a-motor-y adventures).

Scullion tells me that he and his friends have accounted for the R.C. policeman who batoned his cousin. They have painted slogans on the pavement in front of the man's house. Two of Scullion's friends have also undertaken to call upon Mrs Policeman and tell her, in no uncertain terms, what they think of R.C.s.

I cannot say that I altogether approve of this treatment of a member of the Royal Ulster Constabulary, on the other hand it is obvious that the Inspector General of the R.U.C. and the Minister of Home Affairs (Mr Porter) have been duped by certain traitors within the ranks, otherwise there would never have been the disgraceful attack upon Loyalists in their homes last Sunday. As Scullion's cousin was merely strolling with some other youths in the vicinity of the R.C. Flats in Unity Walk when this R.C. policeman set upon them, I really cannot find it in my heart to condemn the lads who are merely exercising a rough and ready justice. (We don't want these R.C.s coming up from over the border and trying to carry out Jack Lynch Law!!!!)

It is interesting that Mr Porter (The Minister of Home Affairs) and the Inspector General of the R.U.C. have taken no steps to dismiss all R.C.s from the force. This would seem to show that Bingham's distrust of that particular Minister may not, after all, be ill founded. We want no quislings selling up our heritage for coins collected from a Roman fountain (or font!!).

An interesting little exchange with Mr Blaney junior in the lift, while going out for luncheon. Thinking to test his mettle once more, I said: 'I see that these Republicans in Derry are still trying to get the Minister to ban the Apprentice Boys' March on the 12th sir. Quite extraordinary, I call it.'

'I daresay, Harland,' he replied, 'that you would not welcome a parade of Roman Catholics around your front door, shouting offensive slogans. Especially if, in the months before, you had seen your area over-run by so-called guardians of the law, breaking windows and using water cannon on innocent by-standers ... and hastening the death of at least one of your neighbours.'

'Aye, but sir,' I said, 'this is our country, we are

entitled to our marches. That is the difference. Derry is our city.'

'Two thirds Catholic population, Harland,' he said. 'Two thirds delicately gerrymandered so that their city is ruled by the Protestant one-third of the population. Two thirds discriminated against in housing and employment. You may find them prepared to take your city from you if you don't watch out.'

We completed our journey to the ground floor in silence.

If I had thought of it in time I would have quoted to him what Dr Russell Abernathy, Governor of the Apprentice Boys of Derry said yesterday (As reported in my morning paper):

'It is a carnival day for Derry and brings a lot of business for traders.' He said that he did not think there would be *'Any feeling'* against the march, which commemorates the relief of the city in 1689. According to my paper Dr Abernathy also said: *'If there is trouble it will be caused by hooligans and drunks ... not the people of Derry.'*

Meanwhile the R.C.s in Derry have taken typical provocative action, forming a defence force to stay in the Bogside and prevent ordinary R.C.s from going in or out to enjoy the celebrations. I suppose they hope that this will provoke Loyalists. Ever since the R.C.s got the government to give in and disband the Loyalists who had been democratically elected to rule over them in the City Council and set up a ridiculous Commission of outsiders (so-called impartial) they have had their tails (tales!!) in the air, spoiling for a fight. If they throw one rock or petrol bomb at our parade on the 12th of August we shall let them have one too!!!! If they didn't like what they got last time, they'll like it a lot less when the Apprentices have finished with them!!!

I presume In-Hume-Ane is at work stirring things up

again, not to mention Burn-a-debt (I call her Burn-a-debt because all the R.C.s have their things on Hire-purchase and when they get burnt the R.C.s claim from our authorities for the loss of their things, and thus escape from their debts (whilst having enjoyed the use of the goods for sometime. Some R.C.s have even destroyed their own goods, I'm told.))

I see there is another article in the *Newsletter* about the R.C. Kennedy family. I should think even the Yanks will have had enough of them by now. Clever Senator Edward has indicated his support for the Civil Rioters over here ... I am happy to say he has since had his come-uppance, and is now totally discredited. Ulster has given more to the U.S.A. than the U.S.A. can ever give to Ulster, and it is about time they stopped raising funds for the I.R.A. over there and acknowledged their debt to our Protestant people!!!

I returned home with this evening's meeting of U.M.P.I.R.E. very much on my mind. I have no idea what Mr Balderwood of Lower Basin St., (The Hon. Sec. of U.M.P.I.R.E.) will have to say to us as he has not had the courtesy to present an agenda. 'Emergency Meeting' is all the intimation we have had from the Hon Sec.—I may say if this is to be another attempt by the committee to weaken the resolve of ground roots members they may find that they have bitten off more than they can chew.

I resolved to speak to Bingham about it.

He was undoing a parcel when I came in, and surrounded by little boys. I waited until the crowd had cleared, and then I saluted him.

'Commandant,' I said. (Bingham is the Area Commandant of A-Certain-Organization-Which-Shall-Be-Nameless) (In case the Republicans should find this little book.) 'Commandant,' I said (Although I should make it clear that I am not, as yet, a member of the

C.O.W.S.B.N.) 'I have a matter of the most pressing importance to communicate to you.'

Then I told him of the trend of affairs within U.M.P.I.R.E., and how several of the members (Myself, McGinn, Williams, Patterson, Turner and Mrs Rivers of Stone St.) felt about it. What we needed, I told him, was the help of someone like himself, a forceful speaker, to put our case at the meeting.

'That's all very well, Harland,' he said, 'but I am not a member of U.M.P.I.R.E.'

I explained to him that membership of U.M.P.I.R.E. is open to all moderate Protestants interested in furthering community life in our province.

'What does Community Life mean, Harland?' he said. 'Your O'Neillism is showing. I for one can have no part in encouraging R.C.s to stay here, taking the bread out of our children's mouths.'

'That's just the point,' I said.

'I'm not that sort of moderate, Harland,' he said, shaking his head.

'Nor I, indeed, Bingham,' I said. 'But I can't say that I agree with you entirely. The purpose of U.M.P.I.R.E. (of which I am a founder member) was to draw together moderate Protestant opinion behind Captain O'Neill in his bid to involve the people.'

'Thank God we're rid of Captain Go-Neill!!!' quipped Bingham. I had not heard this before and thought it very funny.

'Involving the people does not mean involving R.C.s as R.C.s,' I said. 'Some R.C.s are prepared to live like us, and those are the ones we ought to involve, provided they are prepared to behave themselves. The Rev. Paisley for instance, has helped more lapsed R.C.s than any clergyman in this city, and that is no reflection on his loyalty is it?'

'Oh some R.C.s are all right,' admitted Bingham. 'It's when they get together you've got to watch them.'

'Exactly,' I said. 'If they would mix with us and partake in our community life everything would be all right: Once we Protestants show a sign of weakening they will nip in and take things over. That's why we've got to make them see that the Protestant community spirit is steadfast as a rock. Not an inch! No surrender! If they see that we are strong enough to deal with them there is no reason why we shouldn't live happily together. The ones who don't like it can go back to the Republic.'

'Right,' said Bingham.

And he agreed to come to tonight's meeting of U.M.P.I.R.E., as an interested observer.

I think I may regard this as a coup!

My potted plant for peace project has also borne fruit!!! The young man from next door (Dermot Murphy) called on my wife Victoria Alberta this afternoon and presented her with a potted plant, which is now displayed in our front window beneath the Union Jack poster. I am interested because he called during the hours of the afternoon when working men are out at their business, which means that he is either a student or unemployed. As he was able to buy the house next door, I presume that he is not unemployed, therefore he must be a student. This, coupled with his name, is a pretty clear indication of the sort of person he is.

A cheerful tea. The Honourable Roland (Whom I shall call Roland, as he permits me to do so) was present and regaled us with a number of tales about the Government Information Service ... some of which were most surprising (Not to say a little ribald). After tea, when my daughter and Victoria Alberta had retired to do the dishes and Mother had gone for forty winks (unfortunately she enjoys her winks in the sitting-room, and insists on bathing her feet in the methylated at the same time) I took the opportunity of pointing out to young Roland that the ladies had been a little embarrassed by his stories, and to ask him to refrain from ribaldry in their presence.

'Old Mrs Harland told *me* some,' he said.

'Mrs Harland is a very old lady,' I said. 'One must make allowances.'

'She still has a fancy man, you know,' he said.

'A what?' I said. 'I am sorry, I do not understand you.'

'Oh nothing,' he said. 'You ask your wife about the man who came to fix the ladder, that is all.'

Young Roland would say no more. I think he realizes (apart from Mother's digressions) that what might be all right in the gay salons of Reading Berkshire falls a little awkwardly on the ears of those of us brought up according to the Good Book. I will say that young Roland took it like a man. We settled by the fireside, the old grizzled A.R.P. man (the son of an honest toiler who dragged himself up by his boot strings until he was his own man in the little shop on the Albertbridge road) and the flower of the English landed gentry, and I think I may say that that fine lad hung upon my words as we talked of cabbages and kings.

It seems that the English Press (particularly the Sundays) have mis-represented events in Northern Ireland. Young Roland expressed himself as quite astonished when I presented him with the facts. He did not realize, for instance, the full import of the recent Papal pronouncement on birth control. I had to explain to him that, far from being a stand against the 'swinging' generation (With which I could not help but approve) the Pope has taken his stand with an eye to the Northern Ireland situation. It should be apparent to anyone that, with His one third of the population *off* the pill, and our two thirds *on* it, it cannot be long before the R.C.s would simply breed us into the Republic, not to speak of bleeding us white with the family allowances. The Pope of course, would love to see an end to our Ulster.

'That certainly explains the business about the pill, sir,' said Young Roland, respectfully.

'Indeed it does, Roland,' I said.

'And what about Londonderry sir?' he said. 'Our newspapers would have us believe that to be a very sorry city indeed, and the T.V. pictures we have seen were quite horrifying.'

'Faked,' I told him firmly.

'Oh but surely sir ...'

'It is a well known fact, Roland,' I insisted, 'though difficult for an English person to understand, that the newspapers and T.V. networks have been infiltrated by left wing sympathizers, who have arranged matters for their own ends.'

'But surely policemen batoning innocent bystanders ...'

'By-standing what, Roland?' I said. 'A disorganized rabble running through the streets of Derry, petrol bombing and looting and robbing the city of its last chance of prosperity.'

'But wasn't there an attack at Burntollet Bridge ... ?'

'Ah,' I said. 'There now, there's a tale. The truth of that little matter is that Loyalists, persistently provoked for a number of days by the carrying of Republican emblems through our areas by armed Republican thugs turned up at Burntollet for a spontaneous and dignified silent protest and were set upon by R.C. members of the R.U.C. and Republican thugs, who beat them off the road. There were, I freely admit, some isolated examples of Protestants fighting back ... but that is the gist of Burntollet. Now the R.C.s have come forward with stories of Fenian women being attacked, and innocent students battered ... innocent!!! ... members of the rebel People's Democracy. Do you know what I call it Roland ... The Papal

Democracy, that's what I call it!'

'I find it all most confusing,' said Young Roland. 'One saw such terrible photographs. Women being beaten with nail studded sticks...'

'Oh yes,' I said. 'I quite agree. Utterly disgusting.'

'Well then,' said Young Roland, with a puzzled frown.

'Tell me Roland,' I said, 'did the pictures have captions? Did it say beside the figure who was being beaten "Innocent student" and across the body of his or her assailant "Protestant"? No Roland! It did not! And why not?'

'Why not?' said Roland.

'Because the captions would have been the other way round,' I exclaimed. 'Loyalists were assaulted and beaten at Burntollet, whilst the police allowed a Republican armed parade to pass! The same Republicans who had earlier broken up a peaceful meeting of the Rev. Paisley's in the Guildhall Derry. All of these events have been misreported and represented falsely.'

'But surely some of them must be true,' said Roland. 'All these reports can't be biased.'

'In any case,' I said, 'if they did get beaten up by our people, it's only what they deserve.'

Roland nodded sadly.

'They complain about discrimination,' I said, 'but they discriminate against *us* in the South.'

'But I thought the Protestants in the South were quite happy.'

'Ah,' I said. 'Roland ... you don't understand, my boy. They *say* they're happy, because they're afraid. No one knows what might happen to them down there if they complained. It isn't Britain, you know. They don't have justice like we do. The Parish Priest rules the roost down there, I can tell you.'

'How do you know?' he said.

'What?' I said.

'If the Protestants down there are afraid to tell you, how do you know they're discriminated against?' he said.

'Ah, Roland,' I said, 'I can see you don't really understand it at all. They have to discriminate against us, you see, because their Parish Priests put them up to it. They aren't all bad people. There are good Catholics too you see, who would live like good Protestants if their Priests would let them. But they won't you see, because their Parish Priests would lose their fat livings if they did.'

'I see,' said Roland.

'So when we discriminate against them up here, we're only getting our own back,' I said.

'But you don't discriminate, do you?' he said.

'Of course not,' I said. 'We're British. But if we did, we would. And anyway if they don't like it here because we give Loyalists houses and jobs in front of those who would betray us into the arms of the Pope, they can always go back to their Republic, can't they?'

'I suppose so,' said Roland.

'You must remember,' I said, 'we fought for Britain in two wars. Fought against the Hun. Some of your best soldiers came from Ulster. Generals. We are loyal. We like things British. They don't. We see to it that everything is fair play and above board, with no heed for class, creed or colour. That's the way it is, and that's the way it's going to be as long as we rule our Ulster. We stand for justice, free speech, liberty of thought, and the pill for all!' I said.

At that moment Angelica Elizabeth came in and, when she heard what I was saying, she had the temerity to interrupt. 'Oh daddy,' she said. 'Do shut up. You make me sick.'

I was about to speak sharply to her for abusing her father in front of a guest when Roland interrupted. 'Now now Angelica Elizabeth,' he said. 'I'm learning a lot from your Daddy Augustus.'

At which ... for reasons I am quite unable to understand ... Angelica Elizabeth burst out laughing and left the room.

Obviously the boy thinks of me as a sort of father-figure.

I introduced Roland to Bingham when he called round, and they had a very civil conversation. The boy has breeding, and reminds me (despite his long or at least longish hair) of my boy Craig, now doing well in California.

The boy later excused himself and went to join Angelica Elizabeth in the backyard. I am happy to say that our daughter has shown a surprising interest in horticulture since her return and is tending our 'Teeny patch' (four by four, with ornamental paving round the outside). She and young Roland seem to enjoy each other's company, and stay out there quite a bit, according to Victoria Alberta. This evening, while Bingham and I talked of the meeting before us, we could hear them chattering and laughing away like two love birds.

Do I hear the distant tinkle of sweet wedding bells?

I certainly would not mind Young Roland as a son in law. He is well bred and intelligent, not the sort of youth to be taken in by the scandal mongers of the Vatican Press Corps!!

I shall have to speak to Angelica Elizabeth after her rude outburst. I must also remember to have my little say with her, before her holiday is up. By the by, I have as yet no idea when she intends to return to her post in London.

On the way to my car (parked outside the boot repair shop as usual) Bingham and I dropped in for a word with our local 'B' Special, William Fullerton. Greeted by Mrs Fullerton at the door, who told us that William would definitely *not* be coming out with us, as he had been on duty every night since Sunday, in addition to carrying on his usual work during the day. Mrs Fullerton (Amelia) is a good woman, and a four square Unionist. I gather that it was at her insistence that William joined the 'B' Specials. Just before we left (Mrs Fullerton had wetted the pot for us) a most amusing incident happened.

Mrs Fullerton suggested to Mr Bingham that he ought to be in uniform like her husband William!!!!!

I could hardly restrain myself from bursting out with the truth!!! Bingham, however, excused himself on the grounds of business necessity. He is certainly very careful whom he entrusts with the secret of his real role in the C.O.W.S.B.N. I am glad to say that he trusts me.

The Lord Carson Memorial Hall in Masonic Street was quite crowded when we got there, and I introduced Bingham (not as a leader of the C.O.W.S.B.N. but as an 'interested Observer') to our Loyalist members; McGinn, Williams, Patterson, and Mrs Rivers. (Turner, I am sorry to say, is in hospital. He had gone to Derry to help our police there resist the rebels, and was set on fire by a petrol bomb thrown by a Republican Hooligan.) We sat, as is our custom, in the corner of the hall closest to the flag, whilst the other members, some fifteen in all, took their places in the body of the hall, and the committee (Messrs. Gordon, Dawkins, Aiken and Major Strain) together with the Hon. Sec. Mr Balderwood took their places on the platform.

We sat back to listen.

Strain got to his feet, addressing us, he said, as an old soldier and also as Chairman of U.M.P.I.R.E. After reminding us of the moderate nature of our organization and aims, he said that he and the Hon. Sec. had taken it upon themselves to call this meeting as they thought it time we (the Ulster Moderates) made ourselves felt in the current situation. He said that it was his opinion, as an old soldier himself and one well qualified to speak, that we should address an appeal on behalf of all Ulster Moderates to the Westminster Government, asking them to suspend the activities of the R.U.C. and replace them with members of the Armed Forces. With that he sat down. There was a stunned silence in the hall. Then Balderwood, his face white, leant across the committee table and said. 'That wasn't what you told me you were going to say, Major.'

'It is nonetheless my considered opinion,' said Major Strain.

'From which I must dissociate myself,' said Balderwood, quickly. 'You said we must discuss the current situation.'

'Well, I'm discussing it,' said the Major.

Mrs Rivers got to her feet. 'Is the Major aware that my husband is a member of the R.U.C.?' she said, exercising splendid control.

'Madam,' said the Major, 'it is your husband's interests I am considering. I do not consider that brave men who are doing their duty should be exposed to the activities of hooligans with petrol bombs.'

'Oh that's different,' said Mrs Rivers, and sat down.

'Here here,' I said. And a ripple of applause followed.

Mr Gordon (of the committee) then got to his feet. 'I think that the Major has now made it plain to us all that no slight to the R.U.C. is intended by his suggestion. He is merely thinking in terms of protecting their interests. And I am sure we would all agree that that is a desirable end.' He sat down.

'I associate myself again,' said Balderwood, with a smile. 'I am afraid that I misunderstood you, Major.'

I got to my feet, thinking it was about time we got on to priorities. 'Gentlemen,' I said, 'I am sorry to raise what may seem to many of you a trivial point, but is it not a fact that this meeting is out of order, in that the matter of correspondence should be dealt with before proceeding to other matters?'

'There is no correspondence, Mr Harland,' said Balderwood sharply.

'I am sorry to contradict you, Mr Balderwood,' I said. 'But there is! I myself addressed a letter to the committee within the past few days. Surely that is "correspondence", and should take priority over the Major's point?'

The Major got to his feet, whilst Balderwood floundered. 'I can assure you, Mr Harland,' he said, 'that your letter has received the committee's attention and consideration. However it was addressed to the committee, and has been dealt with by us. This is a general meeting called to debate the particular circumstances in which we find ourselves. We cannot debate committee matters in general.'

'Why have a committee?' said one of the others, a Mr Grene from Warsaw St.

'I am sorry,' I said, 'but I consider that my suggestion was germane.' And I proceeded to outline it, despite the protests of the Hon. Sec. and the Chairman. When I had finished there was a respectful silence.

'Well,' I said. 'I think we should vote on it.'

'This is most irregular,' said Balderwood. 'Another motion is before the house.'

'Your procedure is incorrect, Balderwood,' I said. 'My Ulster Bands for Peace letter should have preceded the Major's suggestion, as it was contained in prior correspondence which should have been laid before the committee.'

'Can we allow a vote, Major?' said Balderwood.

The Major shrugged.

Mr Aiken (of the committee) then spoke out. 'I think we may allow a vote, as it seems to be a matter of such importance to Mr Harland.'

'Thank you, Mr Aiken,' I said. 'You at least are a

gentleman.'

'Thank you Mr Harland,' said Aiken. 'However, in fairness, I think I ought to say that your committee has already considered this motion, have we not Mr Chairman?'

The Major nodded.

'It is also fair to say,' Aiken went on, 'that your committee did not decide to act on Mr Harland's suggestion, as we do not feel that an "Ulster Bands for Peace Concert" would be conducive to Civic stability at the present time.'

'I think I take exception to that remark, Mr Chairman,' I said.

'Your objection is noted, Mr Harland,' said the Major.

'Well,' I said, 'Well.'

I am happy to say that Mrs Rivers was on her feet at once. 'Is the committee suggesting,' she said, 'that Ulster Bands might disrupt the peace?'

'Mrs Rivers,' said the Major, 'we must accept that certain ... traditional ... tunes could, in certain circumstances, be regarded as inflammatory.'

'Is the Committee suggesting that Loyalists should not be allowed to sing Loyalists' songs in their own City?' snapped back Mrs Rivers.

That caught them!!!! They fairly floundered, I can tell you.

'I suppose,' I said, with heavy sarcasm, 'that the Committee would therefore stand shoulder to shoulder with the Derry Bogsiders, who are objecting to a traditional day of carnival in that city, on the grounds that a happy celebration is inflammatory!'

'We shall be lucky to get through Tuesday the 12th, that's all,' said Aiken.

'Unless the troops are called in,' said the Major. 'Perhaps we could get back to that point.'

'Yes, perhaps we could,' said a firm voice, and Bingham sprang to his feet. 'I wish to make it clear that I am here as an onlooker, as I find the O'Neillite Unionism of your organization a giveaway to Popery, and would not wish to be associated with it. However I do think I should point out to you that any call for troops will, in all likelihood, lead to control of our province from Westminster, and the Death of the Stormont Parliament for which our fathers fought. If that is what you want, you are at liberty to call upon the Westminster Government to intervene. I am sure Harold will leap at the opportunity.'

Bingham sat down.

'Well spoken,' said Mr Williams.

'I don't think Westminster control would be such a bad thing,' said Major Strain.

I am glad to say that the meeting pretty soon put him straight on our feelings on that little matter. Stormont is ours and Stormont stays, we told him. I then rose and proposed that we reject the Major's motion out of hand. I am happy to say that my motion was carried, with only the Major, and two or three fellow travellers voting against.

'In that case,' said the Major stiffly, 'I am sorry to say I must resign my commission as your Chairman.' And he stalked from the room.

There was silence. Then Balderwood said. 'Me too.' and left after him.

'I think you are making a mistake, gentlemen,' said Mr Gordon.

'And lady,' said Mrs Rivers.

'Oh hell,' said Gordon, and he and Aiken quit the platform.

It was the feeling of those of us who remained that U.M.P.I.R.E. should not be reconstituted. Instead, on the motion of Mr Bingham, eleven of us including the old-faithfuls (McGinn, Williams, Patterson, Mrs Rivers and myself) have formed ourselves into a Protestant

Defence Unit, and Bingham has undertaken to put us in touch with those who can use our talents best.

I am proud to say that I have been elected Captain of our Unit, directly answerable to Bingham. I shall do my best to be worthy of the honour. Mrs Rivers is to be my second in command, though naturally she will not be expected to take part in actions against the R.C.s (should these prove necessary).

It is like the old days all over again, when we (in the A.R.P.) put old Adolf's nose out of joint.

SATURDAY, THE NINTH OF AUGUST

My first day as Captain of the Boyne Protestant Defence Unit, which is the name I have chosen for our group, founded upon the backbone of the now defunct U.M.P.I.R.E. organization, which had suffered a take-over from left-wing and New Ulster Movement Elements. Although at one time I did flirt with the idea of joining the New Ulster Movement, Bingham says (And I agree with him) that it is no more than a front for so called progressive O'Neillite policies, which have already been discredited by red fellow travellers. Surely it should be obvious to all Ulster moderates. The N.U.M. has made several public pronouncements favouring a give-away to Roman Catholic demands, and has become a rallying point for red and leftists who are, for one reason or another, afraid to tack their true Republican and Romanist colours to the mast. An example of this is the demand that the Orange Order should be divorced from the Unionist Party. As the Orange Order stands first and foremost for the Preservation of the Protestant Faith this is clearly an incitement by N.U.M. to R.C.s, and the implied criticism of Major Chichester-Clark and his Ministers is not to be tolerated. I am sorry to see that some of our new M.P.s are *not* members of the Order; but these people crept in on the coat tails of the misguided Terence O'Neill, and one hopes that Loyal Unionists will give them short thrift at the next election. Bingham refers to the N.U.M. as N.U.M.B. (Numb) which I think is very witty, and typical of the man.

My first act as Captain was to circulate a memorandum to all my officers and other ranks (Mrs Rivers is my officer) asking them to obtain as many milk bottles as possible from Loyalist Sympathizers and bring these to the store behind Bingham's shop, together with whatever rags they can muster. I gather that C.O.W.S.B.N. can provide petrol in plenty, though Bingham says that he may later have to call upon our group for assistance in preparing the bombs. Fortunately Bingham's Uncle owns a sand-pit, so there should be no difficulty where that is concerned.

A busy day then, but marred by domestic trivia. The morning began pleasantly enough. Conversation around the breakfast table has reached quite an elevated level with the advent of Young Roland. At last I have a man of my own mettle to swop opinions with. Not since the days of my son Craig has conversation flowed so fast and furious across the creaking board. This morning the boy, off his own bat, came up with a proposal which quite delighted me.

'Mr Harland,' he said, 'or if I may be so bold as to call you, "Daddy Augustus"...'

'Indeed you may, my son,' I said, warmly ... at which my daughter (quite inexplicably) went into a deep fit of giggles, so much so that Mother had to pat her upon the back to prevent her from choking upon her toast. (Her sixth piece, no less!)

'Daddy Augustus,' Roland continued, 'listening to you explaining the Ulster situation has been a revelation to me. I am sure that your thoughts will be of inestimable value in helping me with my work for the Government Information Service.' (At which Mother muttered something which I could not catch, although I fancy it was not a *proper* remark to give vent to in the presence of my daughter. I *really must* speak to Mother.)

'Thank you, my boy,' I said.

He then put a startling suggestion to me. As my house guest (and therefore, he inferred, being unable by the rules of etiquette to offer me cash in return for hospitality) he felt himself indebted to me, and had been hunting around for some way to thank me. After much thought, he said, he had hit upon the idea of providing me with a new Union Jack, and a flagpole from which to fly it!!!!!

Need I say that I was delighted!!

Furthermore (he said) if I would walk to the window and look out into my backyard, I should see it fluttering proudly there!!!

And sure enough, there it was, a solid metal flagpole set beside the wall of our outside W.C. (now seldom used, as our terrace has been modernized) and from the top of the pole the flag of the Union of the British Nation fluttering, as it fluttered over Agincourt and Crecy. I said so, thanking him.

'I don't think it did, Daddy Augustus,' said my daughter, and collapsed in giggles again.

I was forced to send her to her room. I am sorry to say that she regarded the whole business of Young Roland's gift to me as a tremendous joke. I am sure I cannot see what is funny about it. I am, however, happy to report that Mother has seen the error of her ways. She seemed very pleased to see our flag billowing out over Boyne Villas, and remarked that she was 'sure it would come in useful for something' ... though this remark was perhaps a little cryptic. Mother and Young Roland seem to have formed quite a close attachment, to judge by the winks and nods that passed between them. I may say they seem strange bedfellows (If one should use such a phrase in relation to one's parent). For my part, if I have any reservation about my splendid present, it is that the flagpole should be somewhat unfortunately sited, but Roland explained to me that, placed where it was beside the W.C., it could be seen from the distant flats, some of which, he told me, are occupied by R.C.s. That is certainly as good a reason as any for flying it there, though I would rather it were at the front.

A splendid gesture from a splendid young man.

Unfortunately my happiness was spoiled by Victoria Alberta, who called me into the kitchen. Apparently she and Mother, for a time companions in arms against me, have had a little dispute. As the account of what had taken place was somewhat garbled, I pulled her up short, and asked for a simple unflustered explanation of her complaint.

'I have done my best to be pals with your Mother, Augustus,' she said. 'But there is a limit to what any woman can take. I have enough trouble with you, without that ... that...'

'Try to be reasonable, my dear,' I said.

'Reasonable,' she said, idly toying with the bread knife, which I felt compelled to remove from her reach and place on a high shelf.

'Reasonable,' I said. 'No doubt Mother has her quirks ... I have my own, I freely admit ... and you have yours. The essence of life is to live in peace together.' This is a dictum of Craig's, and the motto of his newly formed White America Organization, which is doing so much good work keeping the Blackies in their place.

Victoria Alberta fell silent. Then she said: 'Your Mother was sick in the back entry last night.'

I confess that, while perturbed for Mother's health, I was bemused as to the relevance of this news to the subject in hand.

'You know her meths?' went on Victoria Alberta. 'The meths she washes her feet with?'

'Yes.'

'She doesn't throw it away when she's finished with it, that's all. She drinks the stuff!'

I was forced to remonstrate with her, as this was

obviously a falsehood.

'Is it?' said Victoria Alberta. 'How do you think she gets so boozed then? You take all her pension to buy your dirty books with, she has no money of her own.'

'I do not know what you mean,' I said, icily.

'Don't you?' she said. 'I've seen those filthy pictures of yours, the ones you keep under the landing floorboard.'

She was of course referring to the collection of magazines I have been building up for the Ulster Decencies League, (a community project of mine which has had to be postponed owing to pressure of work). I explained this to her, quietly.

'Oh don't bother to cover up,' she said. 'I'm glad something excites you. You obviously lost interest in me a long time ago.'

'That is not true, Victoria,' I said.

'If I walked around with my knickers off and a pair of black suspenders you'd think I'd gone mad,' she said.

'Indeed I should,' I said, severely. 'But, as I have already explained, those pictures are part of my community project.'

I am sorry to say that Victoria Alberta did not seem to believe my explanation. Shortly afterwards she went to bed, leaving me to undertake our weekly shopping trip to Supermac alone. This was an inconvenience to me, and took no regard for the burden of responsibility cast upon me by my new found rank in the Boyne Protestant Defence Unit. However it gave me time to compose my thoughts, and to prepare myself for a heart to heart talk with Mother. Whilst I am sure that Victoria Alberta is mistaken about the methylated spirit, there is still the question of Mother's language to discuss. I may say that, in the last week, I have been in touch with a number of suitable establishments for older persons in an endeavour to find a billet for Mother, but I regret that I have not yet been able to secure one. I am beginning to wonder if that woman at the Gentlefolks has been passing the word around amongst her friends, in an attempt to victimize Mother. I would not put it past her.

I am sorry to say that the trip to Supermac led to further difficulties. I had, I thought, completed my purchases satisfactorily (although I omitted the Meths, which had been added to the list in a hand which was not my wife's!) However, upon my return home Victoria Alberta reported that I had purchased a washing powder of an inferior type and one, moreover, which does not supply the coupons she is collecting for a set of nickel plated spoons. To calm her (she was much overwrought by events) I drove to Maynards, who kindly supplied me with three packs of the correct brand, although they regretted that they were unable to accept the packs already purchased in part exchange. Unfortunately the new packs turned out to be in the wrong coupon series. Victoria Alberta says that we do not need a T.V. snack table, as we no longer have a T.V. (Owing to Mother's sitting upon it) and it seems that the makers will supply only T.V. snack tables on these coupons. I have told Victoria Alberta that I shall write to the soap company about their marketing methods (which I consider to be unfair discrimination, as I am not satisfied that sufficient stocks of individual coupons are made available in Ulster) but I do not hold out much hope.

I went to speak to Mother, but found her indisposed. She says she has broken her foot, although I cannot imagine how she managed it. This raises a delicate matter of toilet facilities, as Mother states that she cannot manage the steps with her 'broken' foot.

'There was one other matter, Mother,' I said to her. 'I am concerned about the language you have seen fit to use in front of my daughter and her guest, Young Roland.'

'What about it?' said Mother.

'I do not deem it suitable for mixed company,' I said.

'You are a remarkable man, Augustus,' said Mother, launching out on a most surprising attack. 'You go to infinite pains to protect your family from anything that sounds unpleasant, whilst at the same time making their lives as nasty as possible.'

'You think so?' I said, coldly.

'Yes,' she said. 'You have reduced poor Vicky from being merely a rather stupid countrywoman to her present state of near hysteria, and you have undoubtedly succeeded in making an enemy of your daughter. Even your son was forced to flee from you ... and that's about the only thing I can say in favour of that dirty little bugger.'

'At least I do not imbibe Methylated spirit from a plastic washbasin,' I said, thoroughly aroused.

Mother chose this moment to produce, from beneath her mattress, the copy of *Garter-Girl* belonging to the Ulster Decencies League, which she set about looking through, at the same time steadfastly refusing to listen to what I had to say to her.

Spoke to Bingham this afternoon (I had come up to the shop to assist him in the task of bottling our Orange-Aid!!!!). He is concerned about the Republican pressure on the Apprentice Boys and says that, if Derry's carnival day is abandoned by the faint hearted, we Protestants will have to take matters into our own hands. In Bingham's company I paid a visit to a family in Rochester St., R.C.s who had wormed their way into a Protestant area. Politely but firmly Bingham told them that they were not wanted in Rochester St., that their neighbours had complained, and that it would be advisable for them to move on before nightfall as otherwise 'something might happen to them, kids or no kids'.

The idea of this operation is of course, to lessen tension all round. If the R.C. family had continued to live in Rochester St. and had later been involved by their Priests in Republican or Socialist activities, there might have been trouble in the street. Now that they have gone there is no reason why Rochester St. should not remain peaceful, whatever the political climate around it. In essence, it seems to me that this peaceful solution to our problems contains the basic answer to all our problems i.e. if they would all go back to the Republic they love so much we would be peaceful up here, and everyone would enjoy full employment and the British Way of Life which we fought for in two world wars against the Hun (and Won!!!)

A telephone call from young Scullion at tea time, to say that the elder Scullion had instructed his offspring to remain in the immediate area of their Street (Cornwallis Parade) to provide the backbone of a defensive organization should marauding gangs of R.C.s attempt to attack innocent women and children in their houses again, or go looting our shops as they did on the Shankill last week-end (and now do as a matter of course in Derry, where the Bogsiders seem to be a law unto themselves, backed by the church of Rome and the Blessed Burn-a-debt.) It appears that Scullion's cousin will also be engaged in defensive operations.

Although inconvenient, this may not be a bad thing. I think it highly probable that, by this time, Blaney will have managed to replace his car, and Saturday night is no doubt convenient for the sort of activities he and Miss Brady indulge in. I had intended in any case to check up on young Scullion and his cousin, to see that they were carrying out their duties properly, but no doubt there would have been some risk of three of us being noticed by the local R.C.s. As it is I will be able to go and have a look around the Bradys' area by myself, and keep an eye out for comings and goings of that young woman after nightfall.

It will be like the old days in the A.R.P. again.

Letters continue to arrive by every post concerning my letter in the *Belfast Telegraph*. (I am sorry to say that the *Newsletter* has not yet printed my letter.) Just at the moment I am too caught up in my duties as Captain of Boyne Protestant Defence Unit to cope with the details of the Ulster Decencies League. I am sorry to say that a minority of my letters still repeat the Public Lavatories filth ... whilst one package at least contained materials more usually deposited there!!!! I am treating these missives with the scorn they deserve.

Young Roland has taken my daughter Angelica Elizabeth to the local 'flicks'. I spoke to Victoria Alberta about it; did she too sense romance in the air? She replied most curiously, something to the effect that there was 'a damn sight too much of it'. But she refused to be drawn further and instead started an argument about who was to be responsible for the emptying of the Elsan I have installed in the attic, as mother is not able to manage the stairs to the bathroom. Naturally mother will not be able to manage it herself, and as I am at work all day, we have a little problem. Victoria Alberta states that she, for one, did not marry me in order to become a (and I hesitate to use the words, but they indicate the difficult relations we are enjoying at the present time) in order to become a 'shit-heaver'.

'It seems my mother is not the only one with a filthy tongue, Victoria Alberta,' I said. (She had previously accused my mother of using bad language.)

I am sorry to say that that closed the conversation, as Victoria Alberta went back to bed, stating that she had a headache.

Not only has someone affixed a padlock to the outside lavatory, but they have locked the padlock as well!!! How strange. I must remember to take up the matter with Victoria Alberta when she is feeling better. Perhaps she is storing valuables out there.

I have found a copy of a rubbishy newsheet entitled *Freedom; Anarchist Weekly* stuffed down the side of the sofa. Among other things it praises the Derry thugs for attacking our police. (Fuzz in the jargon of this rag-bag.) Of course we came across this sort of propaganda in the war with Lord Haw Haw and his friends. The only thing I can say in favour of the publication is that it, too, hits out against the R.C. Kennedy family.

I wonder what religion these Anarchists are? Probably they are Godless. There would seem to be a promising field for some of our Evangelists among this rabble, who would be better turning their faces towards the cross. I suppose as the Captain would say, there is no reason why some Anarchists should not live like good Protestants, once they have been shown the error of their ways. At the moment they are living like R.C.s brawling and looting in the streets, and attempting to blame Loyalists.

I cannot think how this publication came to be in our house. I am sure that Victoria Alberta would never countenance such a thing, if she knew of it and, although my daughter is headstrong and has, on occasion, been seen to mix with company which might, at best, be described as undesirable, she does not dabble in Republican and Socialist filth. I should say this publication came straight from the Vatican, via Moscow and Peking. 'Anarchist' should be spelt 'Anti-Christ' ... and we all know whose Papal N-uncle that is!!!! Young Roland of course is not the sort to mix with rebel-rabble (!!)

I am inclined to the view that *Freedom: The Anarchist Weekly* may have been brought into my house by the workman who repaired the attic stairs. Concerning the visit of this person there is still a mystery which I have not been able to unravel. It appears that he and

Mother had words.

Angelica Elizabeth and Young Roland have taken to visiting my Mother in the attic. I cannot say that I am happy with this arrangement. I have still to have things out with Angelica Elizabeth, and I sense that she is attempting to influence Mother to take her part, as witness the outburst while I was reprimanding Mother about her language.

I have removed those publications which are the property of the Ulster Decencies League (as yet unfounded) from their place beneath the landing floorboard. Although, by rights, I feel that Mother should return *Garter-Girl* to the League, I have decided not to ask her for it. I shall remove it quietly, when a suitable occasion presents itself. I may say that most of the young women in these publications give the lie to tales of living off the bread-line ... their bodies are certainly healthy, not to say over-fed ... so much for discrimination against R.C.s and Socialists. If I had my way I would yank off their suspenders and spank their R.C. bottoms in public!!!! That would teach them what we think of young R.C. women who flaunt their bodies in open indecency against God's Word. Craig tells me that things are even worse in California where hippies and nudists run wild in the streets and flaunt their unwashed selves before all comers. Craig tells me that he has not actually seen any of these naked people himself, but he knows what he would do to them if he did. Especially the Blackies.

TUESDAY, THE TWELFTH OF AUGUST

I am sorry to say that I have spent the past two days in hospital, where I was admitted early in the morning of the Lord's Day. Things have come to a pretty pass when a British Citizen (with war wounds to prove it (to my eardrums) (Although the powers that be have yet to acknowledge them) sustained when I was in the A.R.P. fighting the Hun) cannot go about his own city on his own business without being belaboured and beaten by Republican thugs and hooligans, living off our family allowances and acting, one suspects, at the request of persons who should know better, by virtue of their positions in the business community.

The facts are these:

At about eight o'clock on Saturday evening I went, alone and unaided, unarmed except for my blackthorn stick (Which I regard as a badge of office. Captain of the B.P.D.U.) into an R.C. area (Wheatfield Avenue and its environs) to check on the movements of a known Republican family, the Bradys. I have every reason to believe that the girl Brady, no doubt put up to it by her parents, is indulging in what I believe is described nowadays as a *liaison dangereuse* with a prominent member of my firm, Mr Blaney the younger, and has so used her influence upon him that the man Blaney is allowing her to practically run the Outer office (Witness the appointment of the lad Scullion to do the monthly figures during my absence, against my well known estimation of the lad's ability (since proved correct) No doubt the Bradys' hope to subtly undermine the firm of Blaney, Aiken and McMaster, as subversive elements they would be glad to see the destruction of a sound Unionist firm. After all if our business community can be brought to its knees by Republican activities such as the affaire-Blaney, it is but a short step to a Republican take-over. No doubt the girl thinks that sound Unionists in the firm, like myself and young Scullion, seeing the course events are taking (With the employment of R.C.s and the continual passing over of deserving persons for promotion (such as myself, only lately promoted to a position which I have defacto, occupied for many years) no doubt she hopes that Protestant persons will leave the firm in disgust. Well she is wrong. We will not give an inch. I had therefore determined, (being dissatisfied with the conduct of the young Scullion and his cousin, whom I suspect of not keeping careful watch (being in effect, more interested in Miss Brady's buttocks than her beliefs!!!) to go to Wheatfield Avenue and observe for myself.))

At about a quarter past ten I arrived in Wheatfield Avenue and parked my car at some distance from the Plough (the public house kept by the suspect persons).

I left my car and took a stroll past the premises, spying out the land. A number of persons passed me, but no one stopped to check my name or religion. I had put on a dirty old coat and a pair of worn shoes, with a green and yellow neck-tie, in order to look like an R.C., and I carried a copy of the *Irish News* stuffed under my arm. It transpired that an alleyway from Dicky St. led up past the back windows of the Plough premises, and I settled on this as my point of operations at a later time. The ground surveyed, I went back to my car. As there were a number of R.C. loots in the offing, replete with hurling sticks (their favourite weapon) I thought it wiser to cruise around the area in my car for a short period, before reparking closer to the Plough.

At half past eleven, as Miss Brady had not returned

home, I decided to make a further reconnaissance up the back alley behind the Plough, and, armed only with my blackthorn stick and my pluck, set forth to so do. As far as I could ascertain the R.C. thugs had by this time moved off, no doubt to some other spot where they were carefully calculating a raid on innocent Protestants asleep in their beds.

I approached the back of the Plough carefully, bearing in mind that public houses of this type often, in open defiance of the law (indeed, on occasion, with the open connivance of the guardians of the law, procured by the application of a generous wash of spirit) remain in business behind closed shutters long after closing hours. In the event, this did not prove to be the case, and I was able to make my way via the saddle of a rusty lambretta on to the wall that marked the rear of the living premises adjoining the Plough. There were lights in several windows, but I could see no sign of Miss Brady or her paramour.

I may say, in parenthesis, that all this activity only goes to show the excellent physical shape in which I keep myself. I fancy that not many war veterans could go climbing walls at my age.

As the wall seemed an exposed position, open to enemy fire from all sides, I lowered myself into the small kitchen garden at the rear of the house, finding my way by means of a compost heap to the heart of the enemy camp.

I may say that I was not solely concerned with Miss Brady in this adventure. It also seemed to me that, as Captain of B.P.D.U. and therefore responsible for the security of Protestants in Belfast I, knowing of the existence of a Republican cell, had a clear duty to inspect their premises for Molotov cocktails or other devilish devices (Not to speak of hidden tricolours). To this end I had a look through their potting shed, and inspected a disused W.C., where I found an empty (and rusty) petrol can. I decided against taking this with me on the grounds of security, although it might later have been of use to the authorities.

Shortly after this a light came on in one of the upstairs bedrooms, which was precisely what I had been waiting for. It occurred to me that a well known public figure such as Mr Blaney the younger could hardly be seen consorting with a Republican whore in areas where he was likely to be recognized and, as the family were obviously encouraging the girl to prostitute herself at the feet of their political Gods, it was not unlikely that their acts of unlawful fornication took place in the girl's own quarters.

Carefully removing a ladder from the shed at the rear of the kitchen I mounted up upon it ... wondering if I too was about to catch a glimpse of Miss Brady's celebrated nether portions ... caught, as it were ... in the act!!!

The curtains at the window towards which I climbed were slightly apart, and peering through them, I found myself confronted by a large naked man!!! ... something of a comedown, after what I had been led to expect! However it seemed to me that there was every possibility that he might be another Protestant caught in the net, and that Miss Brady would shortly join him, so I settled into watch, stepping from the ladder on to the roof of their kitchen.

I am sorry to say that this proved to be my undoing.

Republicans, being by nature a feckless people, do not attend to their property as we Protestants do. I am sorry to say that when I placed my full weight upon the roof of their outside kitchen, the roof gave way, and I came crashing through it ... or at least my right leg did, for fortunately I managed to maintain my balance upon the remains of the roof.

The window of the room outside which I had been perched shot up and the large man peered out ... in his

Birthday suit!!!

'Bloody little bastard!' he exclaimed, and stepped through it on to the roof ... which promptly gave way ... in fact the entire ramshackle structure collapsed around us.

Quick on my feet as ever, I was more than a match for him, and managed to struggle clear of the wreckage and would have escaped altogether had I not, in my excitement, mistaken a dark patch of wall for a gap and sprang straight against it, with the unfortunate consequence that I was slightly stunned, and staggered backward to find myself upended in the compost heap (previously mentioned) with the large man belabouring me with a yard brush, and calling out for his neighbours.

Need I say more? Those Republicans are animals!! They do not waste time with the R.U.C. and the normal processes of the law, dear me no. A gang of those ruffians provided their own judge and jury and rough and ready 'justice' (so called) on the spot. If you please, they regarded me not as a political prisoner, but as a Peeping Tom!!!! I may say that I have more to do with my time than to peer through windows at naked Republicans ... the fat man later identified himself as the very Mr Brady who is responsible for the existence of our Miss Brady. In any event, I was set upon by these thugs and soundly beaten within an inch of my life ... to such an extent that I have no coherent memory of subsequent events. Suffice it to say that I was admitted to the hospital at two thirty on the morning of the Lord's Day, suffering from severe concussion, with my ribs badly bruised, and a broken wrist, not to mention being generally black and blue.

It is all most unfortunate.

I have, of course, been interviewed by the R.U.C., but I have decided to keep mum. It seems to me that these R.C.s might well make much of the fact that I was caught in the back of their premises, and accuse me of Peeping Tom activities. Of course, anyone who knows me would immediately laugh away such suggestions, but I have to think of my wife and children, and they might find the subsequent unravelling of the truth an embarrassing process (especially in the light of the current soft approach to the R.C. community by our authorities. It seems that it is as much as a Protestant can do to receive the most elementary redress for his wrongs, while the R.C.s can get away with anything). No. There is a better way for a Loyalist to get justice from these troublemakers, who think they can lay about them without redress.

I refer, of course, to the B.P.D.U., affiliated to the C.O.W.S.B.N. of which Commandant Bingham is our local organizer. Now that it has become obvious that even the Loyal Orange Order has been infiltrated by leftist elements (The arch traitor O'Neill (who for a time duped even me) is a member). The Order has gone so far as to deny that which is common knowledge i.e. that Romanists attacked the Junior Orangemen last week!!! Their statement is in line with those issued by Papists!!! What are Loyalists to make of that? Obviously the Orange Order is facing a Republican takeover. How much more are we to give to these people? Will their demands never be satisfied? Of course it was following the brutal and unjustifiable attack upon the Junior Orange Procession that Loyal Protestants took the law into their own hands and turned upon the Romanists in the Unity Walk flats and showed them that we would not stand aside and see our (traditional and in no way provocative) parades assailed. To deny the attack upon the parade is to suggest that Loyalists attacked the flats without being first provoked by Republican Thugs ... an obvious slander. I shall have to speak to Bingham about the Orange Leaders who issued this statement. Clearly they should find their places upon his list. In any event I shall lay my case before Commandant Bingham, and I am sure that we will swiftly find a means to mete out justice to the Republican Bradys!!

My short stay in hospital has not been a memorable one!

Victoria Alberta and Young Roland visited me once, my daughter not at all.

Mrs Rivers came on Monday, to inform me that she had taken temporary command of the B.P.D.U. during my illness. I asked her upon whose authority she had acted and she said, 'On my own'. I must say this does not bode well for the strength of the organization. I shall have to speak to Commandant Bingham about having her replaced.

I am worried by the little head set things in hospitals. The one by my bed was so adjusted that it would receive only the music programme, thus cutting out our own local branch of the British Broadcasting Corporation.

I discharged myself this afternoon and returned home, to find things in a state of turmoil ... only to be expected when the Captain is absent from the bridge.

Mother's Elsan had not been emptied since Saturday.

My daughter Angelica Elizabeth has barked her shin on the step-ladder leading from the kitchen roof (used to approach the master bedroom now that the passage is blocked by Mother's steps).

There has been some delay over Young Roland's appointment to the Government Information Service. The boy is disappointed, but bearing up under it like a man.

I called with Bingham and outlined what had happened to me. I must say he took it very coolly.

'Well,' I said, 'what steps will the B.P.D.U. take?'
'None,' he said.

'Why not?' I demanded.

'Because the hour is not opportune,' he said.

'I am sorry,' I said, 'but I do not see that.'

'Harland,' he said, 'have you no understanding of the situation?'

'Indeed I have an understanding of the situation, Bingham,' I said. 'The situation is that I have been beaten by Republicans in the streets of a Protestant city. That is not good enough.'

'Harland,' he said, 'you must take my word for it that we have, in preparation, a massive plan to teach these thugs ... all of them, not just those who assaulted you ... a lesson. All that is needed now is some spark to set it off.'

'I don't understand,' I said.

'Harland,' he said, 'today there is a parade in Londonderry. A Loyalist Parade. If there should be any incidents there, Protestants will be prepared. On Friday the rebellious order of Hibernians will parade. On the 16th the Rev. Paisley will parade the Streets of Newry.'

'So?' I said.

'So there will be incidents, Harland,' he said. 'And following the incidents, the Protestant people will arise in their wrath and teach these R.C.s a once and for all lesson.'

'How do you know?' I said.

'Because, Harland,' he said, 'we shall see to it that they do!'

'You mean ... you have it all organized?'

'I do not, Harland,' he said. 'I mean merely that the weapons are available, and certain organizations exist on our side to counter the activities of lawless R.C.s, should they threaten the Protestant people. Once our people are on the march these organizations will provide a spearhead, nothing more. We cannot act without the support of our people.'

'Oh,' I said.

'How shall I put it?' Bingham said. 'Look ... if there is disturbance in the streets, might it not be that under the cover of that disturbance it will be possible for Loyalists and others to take direct action against known Republicans without the intervention of the police? And if this is the case, should we not be prepared to do so? Have we not a duty to be prepared? And is one of our preparations the making up of a list of persons to be dealt with?'

'I suppose so,' I said.

'Right,' he said. 'Your friends the Bradys are on it.'

'What will you do?' I said.

'I don't know,' he said. 'Burn them out, I imagine.'

That should settle their Republican hash. I am much impressed with the depth of Bingham's political thinking. Obviously we have to teach the R.C.s a lesson, and yet our R.U.C. would be honour bound to intervene if R.C.s were openly attacked. However, when the trouble comes (And Bingham seems confident now that it will) we should be able to mop them up most effectively.

I remain suspicious of the R.C. couple next door. Mr Dermot Murphy is not the sort of person I wish to have as a neighbour in these times flower pot or no flower pot.

I think I shall take steps.

I have just heard the news that Republican Thugs from the Bogside have attacked the Parade of the Apprentice Boys of Derry!

WEDNESDAY, THIRTEENTH OF AUGUST

Well, the Republicans have done it now!

The Bogside in Derry has proclaimed its own little Republic. They set upon our parade yesterday (A carnival occasion, which brings business to the town and happiness to all the people) with their petrol bombs (they captured a petrol pump and filled bottles from that), sticks and stones and everything they could lay their hands upon. Steel tipped cudgels, garden hoses, pick axe handles and bottles of ammonia were used against the R.U.C. who, aided by Loyalists again and again attacked the Republican barricades, armed only with C.S. gas bombs. Ivan (the Terrible) Cooper I am glad to say had his head split open and had to be taken to hospital, but Burn-a-debt is there doing just that. The whole of Derry is ablaze.

Of course rebel spokesmen are out on all sides, accusing our police and Loyalists of acts of cruelty. What they don't seem to realize is that this is war! We shall not stop now until the last R.C. has got out of Ulster. We shall show them what cold Protestant steel tastes like in their guts!

As my *Newsletter* says this morning, the Real Minority in the Community are Malcontents and Irresponsibles who have brought this all about ... they don't say so, but I know they mean R.C.s, who have never been content to live within the law like good Protestants.

Women and children are out fighting in Derry, keeping the ammunition lines going to their men. I expect In-Hume-Ane is in the middle of them, egging them on as always, and 'Demon' McCann the Anarchist. There has been fighting in other places. Civil Riotsers are determined to hold the Bogside against the forces of law and order, and they want their Republican fellow travellers to get out on the streets of other towns. If they do come out, we shall give them short shrift, I can tell you.

I went to Bingham's shop at once this morning, and reported for duty.

'What duty?' he said.

'Well,' I said, 'I thought we could go out and burn those Bradys.'

'Have a titter of wit, Harland,' he said, (which I must say I thought was not a reasonable comment). 'There's plenty of time yet to clear the Free-Staters out of it. But not in broad daylight, and not until the boys get going. Once the people are out on the streets we can play our part. If we went up there now we'd only get arrested.'

He is probably right, although it is a sad commentary upon the R.U.C. that Republican thugs like the Bradys cannot be put in their place by Loyalists without the police interfering. The R.U.C. were happy enough to have our boys join in their baton charges on the Bogside. There was no talk of going easy on the Republicans then. Can they wonder that Loyal Ulster Protestants are losing their faith in the police force?

I arrived at work a little late, to find myself dragged over the coals by the whoremonger of the Outer office. It appears that Victoria Alberta had neglected to inform the office that I had been injured by Republican thugs while only doing my duty. I explained this to him in guarded tones. (As I did not want him to connect my injuries with anything he might have heard about the Bradys' supposed Peeping Tom.)

'A man of your age should know better than to be out fighting in the Streets, Harland,' he said.

'Well, Mr Blaney,' I said, 'it seems to me that with these Republican and I.R.A. men waging open war against our Government it is the duty of every Ulsterman to be out there fighting for our faith and the Constitution which has stood us in such good stead these many years. I think that it is the least we can do.'

'Do you, Harland?' he said. 'Do you really believe that fighting with Roman Catholics is your duty as a Christian?'

'I hope I am as good a Christian as the next man sir,' I said.

'I hope you are too, Harland,' he said. 'But why, if you are so keen in your Christianity, can you not live in peace with your neighbours? What happened to the Community Spirit Captain O'Neill did so much to foster?'

'O'Neill was a traitor to his creed and class sir,' I said. 'A willing tool of the Republicans.'

'My God, Harland,' he said. 'I am heartily glad that I am no longer a Unionist.'

'I realized that you had left the faith sir,' I said. 'Otherwise you would not act as you do.'

He seemed taken aback. 'I'm sorry Harland,' he said, getting his papers together. 'I'm afraid I do not understand what you are talking about.'

I decided the time had come to speak out.

'You are no longer a practising Protestant sir,' I said, without unflinching. 'You no longer support our party.'

'It is possible to be a Protestant and not vote Unionist, Harland,' he said.

'It is not, sir,' I said. 'Our faith is in the Union. We defend the Crown and we defend our faith.'

'And where does it say that in the Good Book you are so fond of quoting Harland?' he said.

'Render unto Caesar,' I said.

'What on earth has that got to do with it?' he

bawled, having quite lost control of himself.

'Only this sir,' I said. 'Some members of staff, and I name no name, some Loyalists amid our ranks are distressed to see that the policy of this firm in relation to the employment of R.C.s has been changed.'

'You mean Miss Brady?' he said.

'I mean Miss Brady,' I said, without allowing a flicker to show that I knew of their illicit relationship.

'Miss Brady is good at her job,' he said.

'Is she, or is she not, an R.C.?' I said (Knowing the answer full well).

He came back with the most astounding reply. 'I don't know, Harland. I never asked her.'

'She lives up the Falls,' I said. 'She went to a Catholic School. Her father keeps a public house. Apart from anything else she looks like an R.C.'

'And if Miss Brady is a Catholic, Harland, what of it?'

'I will speak plainly to you sir,' I said. 'As an old employee of the firm, I think I owe it to Blaney, Aiken and McMaster to give clear warning that certain persons may be forced to take certain action against these premises, should Miss Brady continue to be employed here.'

'Is that a threat, Harland?' he said.

'It is a statement of fact sir,' I said. 'We do not like R.C.s in Ulster. You ought to know that.'

'Who sent you to say this, Harland?' he said.

'Oh, a little bird sir,' I said. 'A little proddy bird.'

And I left him there to consider it.

I am happy to say that when we came back from lunch it was to discover that Miss Brady is no longer with us. A temporary is to be engaged, and I think I may say without fear of contradiction that she will not be an R.C.

Evidently her whoring had not given her the power over him which she thought. I am glad, for the sake of

Blaney, Aiken and McMaster. I feel that I have done my duty by my workmates, and the people of my country, Great Britain.

Scullion tells me that he and his cousin have been recruited by an organization on the Shankill Road. I congratulated the boy upon his loyalty, but cautioned him that these things were not for the ears of all, especially in the offices of a man like Blaney. Then I bethought me of Mr Dermot Murphy and his lady wife, perched in No. 10 beside me.

I have set things in motion for this evening.

I fancy Mr Murphy will not be pleased.

Home. The fighting has continued. Mr Bingham has called a meeting of the B.P.D.U. (I may add without consulting me. As I am the B.P.D.U. leader I think he might have moved through the proper channels and contacted me.) However, it is done now, and perhaps it is just as well, as certain members may still be under the misapprehension that Mrs Rivers is their Captain (As I had, so as to speak, been wounded upon active service). I shall take control of the meeting Bingham says. (I should think so too!!!!! After all, a Captain is a Captain, and he is, so as to speak, only a delegate from C.O.W.S.B.N.)

Bingham is very concerned about a pirate radio which has been operating in the early morning in our area. Operating under the name of Radio Waterloo it has been putting out Republican and Socialist propaganda, and exhorting the Civil Riotsers to cause disturbances throughout Belfast.

I have agreed to come down to Bingham's shop at 1 a.m. to listen to this pirate radio. We will then discuss whether any steps can be taken by local Loyalists to curtail the operation of this 'Radio Waterloo'.

I am happy to say that the Minister of Home Affairs has taken steps to ban the outrageous and provocative parade planned by the Hibernians for tomorrow (Thursday) in Dungiven. This is a town with an unfortunate record, where Orange parades have in the past had trouble with R.C.s who live there. As in Derry, they think that because it is their town numerically (because they have allowed very few Protestants to live there) they should be allowed to stage provocative parades through it. Of course it is not their town, it is in Ulster, and therefore belongs to the people of Ulster, the Protestant people. This is particularly true of Derry, which is why we have insisted on maintaining political control there. Had we allowed the Republicans to take it over they would have sold Our City to the Pope there and then. Derry has always been a jewel in the Protestant Crown and always will be. The Queen rules in Derry, and no R.C. is going to say otherwise.

We are The Protestant People!!!!!

R.C.s Out!!!!!!

We had a somewhat heated discussion at tea, on the subject of R.C.s in Ulster. I am afraid that my daughter, having mixed with many undesirables, is all too prone to see their side of things.

'Daddy,' she said, 'do you deny that Catholics have been deprived of jobs and opportunities down through the years?'

'Why should we deprive them of houses, my dear?' I said, patiently.

'Because votes in local government elections are given to ratepayers,' she said. 'No house, no vote.'

'That is true,' I said. 'We do not see why those with no stake in the community should be allowed a vote.'

'So you keep Roman Catholics out of council houses?' said my daughter.

'Sweetening,' I said, 'your daddy knows best. By the very nature of their faith, Roman Catholics cannot have a stake in our Community. The Pope does not recognize our Constitution. R.C.s want only the overthrow of our state. Why should we give them houses so that they can vote us into the Republic?'

'The Cardinal has acknowledged the Constitution, Daddy Augustus,' my daughter insisted. 'As he says himself ... "in letters half an inch high in the *Belfast Telegraph*".'

'Has he, Daddy Augustus?' said Young Roland, to whom I fancy this statement came as something of a revelation.

'Ah,' I said. 'Ah. I see you have not been reading between the lines.'

'Well, has he or hasn't he?' my daughter demanded.

'Angelica Elizabeth,' Victoria Alberta warned (as my daughter was growing a little over excited).

'Of course he has!' I said. 'They'll say anything in the papers, these Romanists. Haven't you ever heard of the Jesuits?'

'Is the Cardinal a Jesuit?' asked Young Roland.

'No,' I said. 'But the principle is the same. They may say they accept the Constitution, these R.C.s, but we know that they don't.'

'I don't think I understand,' said Young Roland.

'Our Province,' I said, 'is based upon the Protestant Faith. That is what our Fathers fought for. That is what King William fought the Boyne for.'

'King William,' said my daughter, 'was on the Pope's side. They said special Masses for him in the Vatican.'

I was forced to send my daughter to her room.

After Victoria Alberta had left us (to cook up mother's snack), I returned to the subject with Young Roland, (who is always ready to provide me with an eager audience).

'The thing people don't understand about Loyalist Ulster, Roland,' I said, 'is that we have fought for the way of life we enjoy. Stormont is important to us, and we intend to maintain it, against all the odds.'

'Oh,' he said, 'I thought your politicians fought against having Stormont.'

'Ah,' I said. 'But you see, it is a question of the Constitution.'

'I thought you hadn't got a Constitution.'

'It all comes back to the Queen being Defender of the Faith,' I said. 'As we Protestants see it, the English Government under Harold Wilson is eroding the very Protestant Faith she's supposed to defend.'

'Catholic,' said Roland.

'What?' I said.

'The Pope gave Henry the VIII the title,' said Roland.

'Don't try to dazzle me with your history, young man,' I said, laughing it off. 'The fact is that Ulster will fight, and Ulster will be right.'

'Right about what?'

'Well,' I said, 'everything we stand for. It all comes out of the Good Book you see.'

'Like turning the B Specials loose on the countryside with rifles,' he said.

I may say I let him see that I was displeased at that remark. It is not good enough for these people to come over here from England and think they know all about it, when all they have studied is a few Marxist textbooks in their schools.

'Of course the B's are a peacekeeping force,' he said.

'Correct,' I said.

'Armed to the teeth, un-numbered, and half trained,' he said. 'With Protestants only as the basic qualification.'

'They are to defend us against the I.R.A.,' I said.

'Damn good thing you've got them, too,' he said. 'I mean if they hadn't been at ... say ... Burntollet Bridge, those I.R.A. thugs and students might have taken over Derry.'

'Right,' I said.

My daughter came into the room. 'It isn't fair Roland,' she said. 'You are to stop baiting him. He doesn't know any better.'

I may say I promptly sent her back to her room again, from which she did not dare to emerge.

Roland left me, and went out to the backyard, where he has been helping my daughter in our little patch. I followed him out, with a suggestion that we should go next door and meet William Fullerton, who is a 'B' Special (though to my mind not a proper one. I had stopped by at his house after seeing Bingham and asked him to call on the Murphys and tell them to get out. I am sorry to say that William maintained that his duty as a constable was to keep them *in*, and as good as threatened me that if any harm came to the Murphys he would know where to lay the blame. That is not the way in which I expect a member of our 'B' Specials to behave.) Roland, however, politely declined the invitation.

My Union Jack still flutters proudly above the outside W.C. Roland mentioned to me, (without being asked) that he was responsible for the lock on the outside W.C. Apparently he has put some valuable equipment connected with his job in the Government Information Services inside it, and wishes to keep it safe. I suggested that we might move his equipment inside, but he says it is probably better there. He also told me that he has run a lead to it from the back kitchen, which he hopes I will not mind.

I told him to treat the house as his own. 'I only hope you are doing good, my boy,' I said.

'Oh,' he said. 'I have given out a lot of information about the Government already.'

This seemed rather cryptic to me, but he would say no more. I gather that his work has now begun, but that it is top secret, and Not-To-Be-Talked-About-With-The-Neighbours. He hinted, although it was no more than a hint, that his work has a lot to do with the flats in the R.C. area, and that my Union Jack is to act as a warning to them that Loyalists are here.

It all seems very sound to me.

The meeting at Bingham's shop was an outstanding success. He has explained to us what we are to do and everything is now in hand. When the hour comes we will not be found wanting. I think it would be inadvisable for me to set down here exactly what Bingham's plans are (in case these notes should fall into the hands of Republicans, but the Boyne Protestant Defence Unit will do its bit when the crunch comes).

I told Bingham of my arrangement with Scullion and his cousin and, some time before the appointed time for Scullion's arrival, we took up position in my front sitting-room, looking out over the front of No. 10.

Scullion arrived some thirty minutes late, which displeased me, however he brought several large youths with him.

They walked up to the door, which was answered by Mrs Murphy, who is dark haired and *very* Papish looking. Scullion's friends crowded in after him, and Mr Dermot Murphy appeared in the hallway, though our view of him was somewhat obscured by the angle from which we were watching.

I do not know what was said, but I imagine that Scullion told him sharply and firmly to get out or else, as we did not want his sort in Protestant Street.

Part one of the treatment.

Amazingly enough, Mr Dermot Murphy had the temerity to come knocking at my door, which was answered by my daughter Angelica Elizabeth, whilst Mr Bingham and I stood breathless in the front room.

Angelica came into us. 'Daddy Augustus,' she said, 'the young man next door wishes to speak to you.'

'Oh yes?' I said. 'And what, may I ask, does Mr Dermot Murphy wish to say to me?'

'I don't know that do I?' she said, pertly.

Bingham and I exchanged significant glances.

'In that case, my dear,' I said, 'you had better show the young man in.'

The young man came in. We put him in the seat nearest the electric fire, with my table lamp turned towards his face. I sat opposite him in the role of host/interrogator, whilst Bingham took up a position framed by the window, just to show him that no funny business would work.

'Well, Mr Murphy,' I said, 'what was it you wished to see me about.'

'Who sent those thugs?' he said.

'Thugs?' I said. 'What thugs? Have you seen any thugs, Bingham?'

Bingham shook his head. 'We have seen no thugs, Murphy,' I said. 'To what thugs are you referring?'

'Mr Harland,' he said. 'When I first came to this street, you went out of your way to make it known to me that you, as a Protestant, were prepared to "tolerate" (and here the young man smiled) "to tolerate" people of different philosophical viewpoints from yourself in the neighbourhood. I am sorry to say that I have now been visited by four thugs, claiming to represent a Protestant Unity Organization, who have ordered me to leave my house.'

'We did not see them,' I said.

'You were watching out the window, Mr Harland,' he said. 'I saw you.'

'We were playing chess,' said Bingham smoothly.

'Indeed,' I said.

'The Roman defence, no doubt,' said the young R.C. and Republican, rising to his feet. 'I suppose you are aware that I shall be getting in touch with the R.U.C. about this, and it will be my duty to report your attitude.'

'Report away all you like, Sonny Jim,' said Bingham. 'But get out, or they'll burn you out!'

'You mean you'll burn me out, don't you?' he said. 'You and your funny friend.'

'Don't call me names in my own home,' I cried, jumping to my feet with the poker in my hand.

'We wouldn't dream of touching you, Mr Dermot Murphy,' said Bingham, taking control of the situation. 'There have always been good relations between Loyalists and R.C.s in this area, whatever provocation may have been offered in the past.'

'I am an agnostic,' interrupted Mr Dermot.

'There have always been good relations between the faiths in this area,' explained Bingham. 'If, I say if, and I and my friend have seen nothing to suggest it, if you have been visited by Loyalists I can only assume that they came from outside this area.'

'The same old story,' said Our Dermot.

'If I were you, Mr Murphy,' I said, 'I should get out, and take your wife with you. And what's more I should get out tonight, before the light goes. Funny things can happen after dark. People never know what hits them.'

Murphy's face had gone quite white, but he stood his ground. 'I have only one more thing to say to you,' he said, 'and it is this. You are an ugly pair. You do not represent anything but yourselves. Not the faith you claim to uphold, certainly not the Crown or Constitution you swear by.'

'We are Ulstermen,' said Bingham.

'Thank God that Ulster will not be judged by you,' said Our Dermot. 'There are other men, good men, men whom you have crucified with your extremist antics. Theirs is the future, the past is yours. You are dead, both of you, dead as the dodo.'

'I think you had better leave us, Murphy,' I said.

He went.

'Well,' said Bingham, 'I fancy we put that young Fenian in his place, though it may be necessary to toast his toes a little if he proves to be stubborn.'

I was forced to point out to him that toasting Mr Dermot Murphy's toes might affect my own property. 'So what,' said Bingham surprisingly. 'This is nothing but a slum anyway. You'd be better off out of it. Say the Fenians did you over. I have friends. I can fix it with the Corporation. You'll get a nice new house.'

To say I was shocked by this suggestion is no exaggeration, and I told Bingham so, in as many words.

'All right, Harland,' he said. 'Have it your own way. If you want to live in a slum, so be it.'

'I have my little garden,' I said. 'I have an indoor lavatory.'

'Three up, two down...'

'And an attic,' I put in.

'And an attic. Damp streaming down your walls. A patch of yard you call a garden, and a back alley behind your house it's safer not to be in at night.'

'I should not like to move out of this area,' I said. 'I have lived here all my life.'

'Well, it's up to you,' Bingham said. 'But the R.C.s aren't the only ones who need better conditions you know.'

'Oh I know that,' I said. 'We Protestants are being held back by them. They come up here and take our jobs and stop this country being what it might be, don't they?'

'Yes, Harland,' he said. 'They do.'

The next incident in the saga of Mr D. Murphy happened when I went to the door to show Bingham out. Who should we see standing talking to Mr D. Murphy but our local 'B' Special William Fullerton.

'Evening William,' said Bingham.

Young Murphy cleared off double time. When he had gone William Fullerton walked across to us.

'Well, William,' I said. 'You'll know us again, won't you? What's the idea eh, boy?'

'Just this, Harland,' he said. 'And you too Bingham. If anything happens in this street, I shall know where to look for the answers, won't I?'

'Listen Fullerton,' said Bingham. 'Are you a Protestant, or aren't you? Because if you're going to take their side you have no business wearing that uniform.'

'I'm a Special Constable, not a rough neck,' said William.

'Och!' snapped Bingham turning away. 'Someone should tell you what it's all about boy.'

'Just be careful, that's all,' said William Fullerton.

He should not be a 'B' Special if he is going to take their side against ours.

It was my intention to end my entry for the day before going to Bingham's to listen out for the pirate Radio Waterloo. However, painful events have taken place, and I feel I must record them. (Also I cannot get to sleep!)

The listening to Radio Waterloo went very well. It certainly must be put a stop to. We received it loud and clear. After the radio had signed off for the night (on returning to my house) I went up the stairs to speak to mother.

I was astounded to hear voices coming from my daughter's room.

As any father would, I walked through the door.

I am sad to say that my daughter and Young Roland were in bed together, with not a stitch on between them.

Suffice it is for now to say that I have ordered the young man out of my house, and in fact stayed up to see him out of the premises. As for my daughter she has locked herself in her room and refuses to communicate with anyone.

Victoria Alberta has gone to bed with a headache.

I am sorely disappointed in Young Roland. It shows, in a way, how much I have been missing my chats with my son Craig that this silver tongued youth was able to take me in.

I have not yet been able to ascertain what ... if anything ... had taken place between them, or if my daughter is still pure. Young Roland, I think to mock me, insisted on conducting all conversation with me in Latin, and my daughter refuses to communicate. If my daughter has been made impure I shall insist that proper steps be taken, or I shall have the young man prosecuted for rape.

I think I shall write a long letter to my son Craig who is in California. With his education he ought to be able to tell me what to do in this terrible situation, which threatens my whole family. I do not know why My God has brought this upon me. When naming my daughter it was a jest between Victoria Alberta and I that her name, Angelica ... meant like-a-Angel (Angellic-a) (The Elizabeth is of course after our Queen) I am sorry to say that our daughter is no angel, but a fallen woman.

So there it is. My world is shattered. My God has forsaken me. My daughter has brought shame and ridicule upon my head before the entire neighbourhood. I frankly do not know how I shall carry on in future.

Could anything worse happen?

I think not.

To have one's daughter grow up to be a harlot is beyond all belief.

It also seems that the Anarchist Weekly magazine belonged to Young Roland, as he spent some time looking for it before he left

THURSDAY, FOURTEENTH OF AUGUST

Well, as we feared, the Republicans have run riot over Ulster. They have been out shooting and looting and throwing petrol bombs and raiding police stations, and Jack Lynch (of Lynch-Law!!) has put his oar in from his safe seat in the Republic! 'We have also asked the British Government to see to it that police attacks on the people of Derry should cease immediately,' says Lynch. 'We do know that many people have been injured and some of them seriously. We know that many of these do not wish to be treated in Six County hospitals.' And so using this as a pretext, he is moving his army up on to our border to make 'field hospitals'. We all know the sort of aid they will be trying to give the Republicans of Bogside and Newry. I am glad to say that Major Chichester-Clark, our P.M., has given Lynch short shrift indeed! Having rebutted Lynch's calls for a U.N. Peace Keeping force in Northern Ireland (We are quite capable of keeping these Republicans and I.R.A. men peaceful ... in their boxes!!!) he says: 'The statement that the police are "attacking" the people of Londonderry is a complete and unpardonable falsehood. Let the appalling figures of police casualties be studied by those who are in any doubt about the source of the aggression. Peaceful citizens do not arm themselves with an arsenal of petrol bombs and other offensive missiles'. I have sent a telegram of congratulation and support to our P.M. on behalf of the B.P.D.U. (though, as the B.P.D.U. is a top secret security project I have signed it on behalf of the now defunct U.M.P.I.R.E. (much the same people anyway, after we sorted out the O'Neillite and N.U.M. (B!!!) fellow travellers.)) However I have not mentioned this to Bingham, as he is too taken up with the business of the C.O.W.S.B.N. to be concerned with supporting our P.M. It is not fair of me to have doubts about Bingham, but I did not like the way in which he referred to Boyne Villas (a superior residential district of terraced houses, many with their own bathrooms and inside toilets, and all with ample space inside) as a slum. If Bingham wants to see slums he should take a trip up the Falls ... those Republicans take no pride in their property. I expect they would be pleased to see it being burned down, as they hope they would be moved to new council flats.

We shall see what we shall see.

For all that, Bingham is a good Protestant, prepared to do his bit for our community.

If 'B' Specials like William Fullerton are going to fall down on their duty others will have to take the law into their own hands.

Which brings me to the events of this morning. I arose early, after (I must say) a sleepless night, having resolved to put the affairs of my daughter and her paramour behind me until the hour of Ulster's need has passed. There will be time enough then to speak to her as a wise and old father should. I have determined that, when the time comes for our little chat, I shall say my say and spare myself nothing. I will not have a whore in the house!!!! I rose alone, as Victoria Alberta insists that her headache has changed to a migraine through worry about 'personal matters' which she is unwilling to discuss. If she will not discuss them how can I help? I shall speak to our doctor about her. However, as I came downstairs to prepare my own breakfast there came a loud knocking at the door. I may say that I did not hurry myself to open it, but took my time, and drew back the latch with a rebuke on my lips.

Imagine my surprise at being confronted by a member of the R.U.C. from our local barracks.

If you please, he had come to threaten me, a loyal Protestant!!! It appears that Mr Dermot Murphy had ratted (No doubt on the advice of our local 'B' fool William Fullerton).

'This is by way of a friendly warning, Mr Harland,' he said. 'To you or any of your friends who may share your inclinations. The police have enough on their hands up the Falls without you poking your nose in. If there is any violence in this street we shall know which house to come to.'

'You seem to misunderstand the situation, officer,' I said, conscious that I was in my pyjama trousers and did not present a very dignified picture to the street. (Most of the neighbours look up to me for a lead, as I am an educated person and occupy an executive position in our industrial drive.) 'I am a Protestant and a Loyalist. You have nothing to fear from me. It is the man next door you should be after. He is an R.C. and a student. I should have thought that the petrol bombs of Bogside and the Falls would have taught you that by now.'

He didn't take this at all well, though as I was sympathizing with the lot of the R.U.C., I think I had gone more than half way to meet him.

'Your activities have come under our notice, Mr Harland,' he said.

'I suppose this comes from living next door to a so called "B" Special,' I snorted.

'Take it as a friendly warning anyway,' he said. 'We don't like lifting prods, but you've got to behave yourselves as much as the next man.'

'You didn't say that when our boys were charging behind you on the Bogside louts!' I snapped, stung by his ingratitude. 'You'll be glad enough to see us next time you are set upon by Republicans and I.R.A.'

'I won't warn you again, Harland,' he said.

After he had gone away I made myself a cup of tea and sat down in the front room, my mind in a turmoil. If this is the way our R.U.C. and 'B' Specials are behaving, is it any wonder that the Republicans believe that they can get away with murder? What is the use of our P.M. appealing for peace for all when our policemen go around threatening Protestants and Loyalists, who are only trying to uphold the Crown and the Constitution which means so much to all of us? Have I not, myself, been beaten into hospital by Republican thugs and Socialist Fenians from Wheatfield Avenue? Where were the R.U.C. then, I should like to know? Hiding behind the coat-tails of Loyalist men and boys who have shown them the way these people should be dealt with ... by force. It is the only logic they understand. When they go to school their Priests beat them about so much (in order to get something into their heads) that they come to resent all sorts and forms of authority.

It is truly staggering to think that William Fullerton, a neighbour of mine for many years, a member of Our 'B' Special Constabulary (formed to protect us from the I.R.A. and Republicans) and a man who is proud to march on the twelfth with a sash on, should so demean himself as to take the word of an R.C. against that of one of his comrades in arms. I wonder what the Master of his Lodge would say. I shall have to find out who it is. This is not what the Orange Order should stand for, I can tell you.

I put on my clothes and went down the street to talk to Bingham about it. He is doing a roaring trade in newspapers these days (because of the Troubles) and could only speak to me between customers.

Bingham was not surprised at the behaviour of our local R.U.C. He says it is well known that despite the fact that Loyalists have been out in Derry and up the Falls and Crumlin Roads helping to keep the R.C.s in check, the R.U.C., apparently on the direction of the Minister of Home Affairs (Porter), have, on several occasions, turned on our side and driven them back. He hastened to add that these, are, of course, isolated incidents, and that the Republican sympathizers among the R.U.C. have by now been marked down by our men so that we shall know how to deal with them when the time comes. He says that he has it on good authority that most of the R.U.C. are prepared to stand shoulder to shoulder with us in defence of the flag, especially as the Republicans last night attacked two Belfast Police Stations at Andersonstown and Hastings Street, and threw a fire bomb through the window of a fireman's vehicle. The R.C.s last night burned down a car showroom on their own Falls Road, and the entire 'B' Special force had to be mobilized for duty (Evidently not William Fullerton. Perhaps they are wise to his Republican sympathies.) We were, in fact, discussing William Fullerton when his wife walked into the shop. She looked most upset.

'Well, Mrs Fullerton,' I said, 'and how is our "B" Special this morning if,' and I gave it very heavy emphasis, '*if*, one can call him that!'

'I couldn't say, Mr Harland,' she said. 'Him and me is no longer indulging in communications.'

'Oh,' I said. 'And why is that?'

'A man,' she said. 'Has to be a man. It's only right to cling to your own.'

'What's he done?' I said.

'He's heaved in his commission, that's what he's done,' she said. 'Ratted on his father and brothers and his friends like yourself, Mr Harland.' And the woman broke down.

It appears that William Fullerton, our ex-'B' Special, disapproved of the activities of some of our more Loyal officers and, among other things, refused to load his rifle. He was very properly taken to task for this, and resigned the force forthwith. Apparently he and his wife have had words, and William has cleared out. We told Mrs Fullerton that we respected her strength of character and would not hold it against her, and we would see that none of the reprisals which might otherwise have been directed against William by outraged Loyalists would affect her.

She was very grateful to us, and is an example to all Loyalists of the courage and tenacity which enabled us to whip the Hun, and will see off the Republicans and R.C. I.R.A. in short time.

No doubt her husband will now join the N.U.M., or offer his support to the discredited Republican O'Neill, who so nearly betrayed our Province into the arms of the Pope.

This morning's news is indeed terrible. Six people are in hospital with gun-shot wounds, fighting continued at its bloodthirsty best all day in Derry. (There is a splendid picture in this morning's *Newsletter* which shows the peace-loving St Burn-a-debt of the Mini Skirt with a brick held over her head, which she is about to use as ammunition against Loyalists.) They have got used to our tear gas up there and are fighting with every imaginable weapon, firing at the police from flats and working, apparently in relays. The tricolour and the flag of the U.S.A. (Which shows where the money to buy their weapons comes from) have been flown high above the Bogside. Houses are going up in flames and Loyalist lives are being put at risk as our boys fight side by side with the police (who should all be told what side they are upon!!!!) Meanwhile a mob of Republicans has taken over the town of Newry (Always a Republican hot bed, and a place where Loyalists are openly discriminated against). Mobs, many of them known to have marched across the border, have sealed off the town, and vandalism on a large scale has taken place. (R.C.s looting again!!!) Mr Patrick O'Hanlon (one of their own M.P.s, and a most undesirable person) seems to have seen the light. He addressed them as follows. 'It is heroic to defend yourselves against the R.U.C. thuggery as they are doing tonight in the Bogside in Derry (Is it indeed, Mr O'Hanlon ... or O'Hellion, as I call him!!! We Prods will see about that, one of these winter nights, when you haven't got your armed thugs around you) but it is no credit to anyone to do as you have been doing tonight.' When even their own M.P.s can see that they are behaving like hooligans and thugs, it is pretty obvious where all honest men should take their stand. I see that In-Hume-Ane has realized too late the dangerous Republican toys he has been playing with, and tried to control his people!!! He is another one who will have to be attended to. In Dungiven the R.C.s have burned down our Orange Hall, and shots were fired. The R.C.s (so keen to have the parade of the Apprentice Boys of Derry called off) are now showing childish ill temper at the decision of Mr Porter to call off their march in Dungiven. It may be traditional, but it is obviously provocative to all good Protestants. I think that (for once) the unfortunate Porter has acted very well. It would not have been proper to call off all marches before Saturday, as this would have meant the end of Derry's carnival day, but now that the Apprentice Boys have proved their point. (That a Loyalist Parade can, and must, be allowed in a Loyalist town, whatever the feelings of the so called Citizens' Defence Committees and their like.) It is obviously a good idea to ban the R.C.s from having a parade in one of their towns, as it would only lead to trouble. We should have had to send men in from the country around to show them that they cannot parade in our Province, and there would have been trouble. No doubt the Minister was aware of this, and it seems a very just decision to me. Ulster is Protestant, and Protestant Parades must be allowed, but there is no reason why we should put up with the activities of R.C.s anxious to provoke trouble.

Bingham has used up all his milk bottles. He says they have gone to a better place, where they will be made use of. He says that our turn will come tonight.

I trust this means that I will be allowed to attend to the little matter of *Chez* Brady. A Republican nest if ever there was one.

Bingham says that he will provide transport, if I will drive. We have selected McGinn and Patterson to travel in the car with us, and the plan is that we shall take a little joyride up the Falls, suitably equipped.

I shall have to stop writing now, as it is time for me to go upstairs and dress for work. The evening's prospect is an exciting one.

Later

What a day this has been. I am tired but triumphant, determined to record the deeds of Our Hour When Ulster called. For all that it has not been a day of unruffled triumph, no indeed. There have been a number of upsetting details, but I shall tell all as it occurred, and leave history to be my witness!!!

'Well,' said our young Mr Blaney, when I walked into his office. 'I trust you are satisfied now, Harland, now that you have burned out the Bogside.'

'Good morning sir,' I said. 'Here are your letters.' Quite as if I had not heard him.

'May God forgive you, Harland,' he said.

'The Lord is My Shepherd sir,' I said. 'I cannot speak for others. However, as you are apparently able to see only one side of this case, I can't say I put your chances very high!!!!'

'What is your side, Harland?' he said.

'I stand for the British connection sir,' I said. 'As did my father before me.'

'You loot and ransack and burn,' he said, growing almost hysterical (it is my opinion that he had drink taken).

'No sir,' I said. 'I leave that to your friends the Republicans and R.C.s.'

'Oh come off it, Harland,' he said. 'The Bogside is a Catholic area. They haven't been burning themselves out, have they?'

'I wouldn't put it past them, sir,' I said.

'It makes me ashamed of being a Protestant,' he said. 'Every responsible churchman in the country has stood up on his hind legs and condemned this sort of thing, every politician...'

'How about Burn-a-debt?' I said. 'She's one of your M.P.s, sir.'

'Not mine Harland,' he said. 'I am a Constitutionalist, and well you know it.'

'You could have fooled me, sir,' I said.

'In any case, Miss Devlin is young and hot headed, and she believes she is doing her best for her people ... you people! For my part, I think she should be taken on one side and told what mobs are all about. But my God, at least she's trying ... and it's you she's fighting for, Harland, you!'

'I don't want Papes on my side sir,' I said.

'Can't you see anything else but Prods and R.C.s?'

'Sir,' I said, 'if we are to preserve our freedom from the Rosary beads, what else is there?'

'Shit,' he said. 'Shit and bugger!!!'

Later, after consultations with Scullion, he and I composed a letter to Mrs Blaney, informing her of her husband's sudden political change of heart, and the reasons for it. I have it on good authority that Mr Blaney the younger was considering standing as an

O'Neillite Unionist in one of our Loyalist areas at the last election. Of course, he would not have got the nomination, as he is not a member of the Order, and his views (Although no doubt acceptable to the brave Captain) are the sort of thing we rank and filers can see through. He and Major Strain (the now discredited ex-chairman of U.M.P.I.R.E. ... which he no doubt hoped to use as a front for Republican Socialist activities) would make fine bed fellows. However when this little lot has calmed down we shall be in a position to sort the Unionist wheat from the chaff. The so-called soft liners, Mrs Dickson, Ferguson, Captain Terence, the suspect Mr Porter and the renegade Minister, Phelim O'Neill will, I should say, have very little chance of retaining the nominations of their Constituency Associations, as they are obviously Republican Trotskyite fellow travellers, whose only wish is to betray Ulster into the arms of the Pope at the behest of Harold Wilson at the head of his so-called Labour Government, in fact a tool of international communism. William Craig, our ex-Minister of Home Affairs, hit upon something when he suggested that Ulstermen might be forced to consider a declaration of U.D.I. If the English are not prepared to stick by the Westminster Confession of Faith upon which the might of our Empire is based they will have to deal with Ulster. They cannot send their armies over here and hope to hold us back, we are Loyal to the Queen and the Constitution and prepared to fight Harold Wilson to the end in defence of our beliefs.

Acting upon Bingham's instructions I have passed on to Scullion a number of addresses in our neighbourhood which might be worthy of a visit and he, in turn, passed on some likely numbers which we might drop in on on our tour tonight. That way, if the man Porter should try to force the R.U.C. into acting against Protestant peacekeepers he will find that any

R.C.s who come scurrying to the barracks for protection will be unable to identify us.

A most embarrassing incident has occurred. Victoria Alberta rang me at the office this afternoon, (Which she has strict orders not to do, as I fear that some of Mr Blaney's Republican contacts may be wire tappers as well) and informed me that the police have called and taken Mother away!!!

It appears that Mother, possibly owing to some mental strain (no doubt occasioned by the treatment meted out to her by the gin sodden procuress Mrs McGrath and her confrère the Rev. (the un-reverend) Dunwoody) has suffered a form of mental breakdown of a particularly unfortunate type. It appears that she had acquired from somewhere (no doubt from the renegade 'B' Special Fullerton) a tattered Republican flag, which she saw fit to fly from the attic window in Boyne Villas, whilst playing Republican songs on the old wind-up gramophone which used to belong to my father. Naturally my wife, when informed of this, attempted to climb the ladder and remonstrate with Mother, but apparently to no avail. Victoria Alberta says that my Mother addressed her in filthy language saying that she had declared herself a Republic, and if they wanted her the R.U.C. would have to come and get her.

I am sorry to say that they did!!

Victoria Alberta assures me that matters were taken out of her hands. It would appear that one of the neighbours got in touch with the nearby station and (as of course they have it in for known Loyalists down there) they came and removed Mother from the attic.

Victoria Alberta also informs me that a furniture van has arrived to take away the Murphys' things from next door. I think we can say that we have safely seen the end of them.

Naturally, I felt it to be my filial duty to go at once

to the local police station and remonstrate with them for removing an old and infirm gentlewoman from the heart of a Loyalist family, when what she was obviously in need of was proper medical attention. This necessitated an interview with the Republican Blaney, but fortunately he was out having one of his expense account luncheons and my request was referred to the Senior partner, Mr McMaster. I told him briefly, without going into the more unfortunate aspects of it, that my Mother had been taken ill as a result of strain occasioned by Republican rioting in the town, and that I wished for compassionate leave for the afternoon to attend to her.

'Indeed, Harland,' said Mr McMaster. 'I suppose we have no *alternative* but to give it to you.'

'I am sorry sir,' I said, 'I do not understand what it is that you are referring to.'

'I will state a hypothetical case, Harland,' he said. 'It is that of employer "A" who is approached by employee "B" who intimates that the pursuit of a certain policy by employer "A" may result in various thugs and hooligans attacking the premises belonging to "A". Employee "B" is known to be an aggressive person, outspoken in his views, and in touch with extremist elements. Employer "A" reluctantly agrees to the condition imposed by employee "B" as he deems that, things being as they are, the authorities might be unable to restrain the aforementioned thugs and hooligans from attacking his premises. The policy objected to is dropped. Later, employee "B", at a time of high tension, approaches Employer "A" with a request to be allowed to leave the premises upon which he is employed during business hours. Employer "A", in the circumstances, is bound to wonder if this may be considered an intimation that Employee "B" knows of certain plans which have been laid in connection with those premises.'

'I am sorry sir,' I said, 'I am afraid that I do not understand.'

'Look, Harland,' he said, 'I'll speak plainly. We are both Protestants. This is an old established Protestant firm. We made a policy mistake, it has since been rectified. If you should know of any element which might be contemplating action against us because of that policy error I trust that you would inform us, and not just take the afternoon off, and let it happen.'

'I know of no such persons, sir,' I said.

'Good,' he said. 'You may have your time off. But please do remind your friends that our staff are their people. Any action against the firm would put you all out of a job.'

It seems the message has got through. I am happy to say that the Senior Partner, at least, has not allowed himself to be swayed by any of Blaney's Socialist nonsense.

I returned home to find that Victoria Alberta had gone to bed with her headache again. It seems to me that my wife is very seldom upon her feet these days. My daughter (sullenly) made me a pot of tea.

'There is no need to slouch around the house like that, Angelica Elizabeth,' I said. 'Any troubles you may have are only those which you have brought upon yourself.'

'There are some things one cannot do entirely by oneself,' she said. 'Or didn't you know?'

'I know that one can remain pure in body and mind,' I said, thinking that it was too good an opportunity to let pass.

'In the family tradition,' she said, pouting.

'What do you mean?' I said.

'Oh,' she said. 'There's you and your dirty books, and Grannie making passes to the man who came to fix the ladder.' Seeing my shocked expression, she continued: 'Didn't you know about that, Daddy Augustus? Grannie groped him ... that's why he left in such a hurry!'

'Never!' I cried.

'She likes a bit on the side, does Grannie. I reckon she fancied Roland as well ... only he preferred me.'

'If that young man has made you pregnant, Angelica,' I said, 'I will have to take a hand in the matter, you realize that?'

'Roland didn't do it,' she said. 'I only wish he had. Roland's not a bad sort.'

'It seems to me that there is no excuse for the high born, like *Mr* (and I emphasized the *Mr*) like Mr Roland Dixon to be taken in by Socialist twaddle, and go around the houses of ordinary people deceiving them and leading their children into paths of depravity.'

'You should meet Pete then,' she said.

'Peter?' I said. 'Peter who?'

'The father of my child,' she said.

There was ... need I say!!! ... a shocked silence.

'Well,' I said. 'I understand that abortions can be obtained under the National Health scheme nowadays, although I cannot say that I approve.'

'That's no good, Daddy Augustus,' she said. 'I've popped already.'

I may say I sat at my table in a state of shock. Not only has my daughter been foolish enough to fornicate with all and sundry, but she has also been foolish enough to spawn a brat!

I will not have her or her child under my roof.

This comes of the foolish stand taken by Victoria Alberta, aided and abetted by the Rev. Dunwoody.

No doubt they knew that my daughter was indulging in foolishness of this sort.

No doubt they will suckle her babe for her.

I shall write to the authorities about the Rev. Dunwoody's brother, who was supposed to be keeping an eye on my daughter.

No doubt they will try to say that it is my fault. Well, I shall tell them that she is no longer my daughter. I have one child only, my son Craig, who has been a great credit to me and is doing very well in California where he has a thriving practice as a Veterinary Surgeon in attendance at a Pets' Cemetery, and has been to dinner with the Governor. He is a credit to me.

This reverie was interrupted by a visit from the R.U.C., who wished to interview my mother!!!!

'Constable,' I said, 'far be it from me to suggest that you are incompetent, but I am given to understand that my mother is at present in the custody of some of your officers and I, in fact, have just obtained compassionate leave from my place of business and was on my way to the police-station to consult with the officers responsible.'

'I'm afraid there has been a little difficulty, sir,' he said.

'If my Mother has come to any harm, officer ...' I began.

'Oh no, sir,' he said. 'Nothing like that.'

'What then?' I said.

It appears that Mother made short work of the officers sent to detain her, and made her escape. The constable explained to me that he had been sent to my home to see if perchance she had returned.

I treated him with withering contempt, pointing out what a shambles the world has come to when several R.U.C. are deployed to hunt down an elderly and infirm Loyalist during a time of National Emergency, when every hand should be turned to tearing down Republican barricades and showing them that we will Defend Our Faith, and when several R.U.C. men, so deployed, allow themselves to be outwitted by the same elderly Loyalist.

He had the grace to blush.

'I consider that you should be ashamed of yourselves,' I said. 'However should my violent and dangerous parent show up, I will no doubt call upon the assistance of the military to hold her for you!!'

And with this sally I closed the door in his face.

Where can Mother be?

Were it not for more pressing matters on hand I should have felt constrained to leave all I was doing and search the streets of Belfast for my elderly parent, however my other duties called.

I was about to repair upstairs to eject my ... the whore of Babylon ... when a loud knocking at the door announced the arrival of Bingham, with the news that the military have taken up position on the streets of Londonderry. The R.C.s have received them with open arms of course. It looks as if our Government has sold us out!!

The Republican plan to use the parade as an excuse for bloodshed has certainly paid off!

The intervention of the troops is, of course, exactly what the Republicans wished for, when they appealed to Civil Riotsers in various parts of the country to come out and make trouble, thus spreading the resources of the R.U.C. and 'B' men and giving Harold Wilson the chance to nip in with his troops. No doubt they consider that they will be well protected behind their barricades in Derry, but there are no troops yet in Belfast, and I fancy they will be taught a sharp lesson.

Certainly, Bingham and I have done our best tonight to teach them one.

It is, of course, not possible for me to give details of the Night When Ulster Called in this little book (No names no Pack drill) in case it should fall into the hands of Republicans or Leftist Romanists. Nevertheless I can say that a/ The car of a certain local shop-keeper (well known as a Romanist) is not where he thinks it is, and has been put to Loyal purposes by certain local Loyalists. b/ McGinn, Patterson, Bingham and I have done our bit, with other Loyalists. Not a milk bottle was wasted, and Bingham has showed us all that he is a man to be respected when behind a machine gun. I fancy a few lines of bullet holes along their walls will make those Republicans sit up. c/ Several R.C. public houses will never raise their shutters again ... as their shutters have been reduced to ashes!!!! (Also the cellar (Actually I use the hole beneath the stairs) at No. 12 Boyne Villas has been stocked up with soft drinks. My comrades in arms, I am sorry to say, did not restrict themselves to 'borrowing' non-alcoholic refreshments. Bingham says, and I agree with him, that R.C. publicans will be worse hit if we take their expensive stock. Nevertheless I have collected myself only some boxes of potato crisps and, of course, my soft drinks 'cellar'!)

The Brady family will not trouble Protestant workers again. Their premises went up with a merry blaze, and Bingham believes that he got a bead on the elder Brady ... thus getting one back for me. I think I may say that that score has been satisfactorily settled!!

We dealt with Scullion's list of addresses, helping R.C. families to move on to places where their beads and holy pictures will be better appreciated. They did the removals themselves ... we merely provided the central heating!!!!

I am happy to say that, on the way home (after leaving the R.C. motor car which had served us so well a-blaze in front of the premises of its owner) (Who will never drive it to Mass again) on my way home from these jollifications I was pleased to note that Scullion and his friends have carried out the tasks allotted to them to the letter. I do not think there will be many R.C.s out and about in Loyalist areas tomorrow ... and those who do return will find a quantity of ash where their furniture used to be. (No doubt they will get it all back from the Government.) (Nevertheless I doubt if they would thank us. Republicans are notoriously ungrateful for little acts of Christian Kindness!!!)

The battle still continues in Belfast, the night sky is lit up with fire, but I fancy that our side is having the best of it!!!!

FRIDAY, FIFTEENTH OF AUGUST

I have been arrested by the R.U.C.

I am to be charged with operating an illegal radio transmitter from 12 Boyne Villas i.e. Radio Waterloo.

It appears that the *Dis* Honourable Roland Dixon was *not* employed by the Government Information Services, but had come over to Northern Ireland at the behest of certain Republican and Anarchist (Anti-Christ) organizations to foment civil disorder. I am ashamed and sorry to relate that, with the connivance of my daughter Angelica Elizabeth (Who has left my home, and with whom I wish to have no further communication), with the connivance of my daughter Angelica Elizabeth, the wretch had set up his 'Radio Waterloo' in the outside W.C. at the rear of Boyne Villas. Not only that, but this pretty pair saw fit to make use of the emblem of our Crown and Constitution (The Union Jack) by flying it from the top of their radio pole, thus misleading me into the belief that they were paying a tribute to my Loyal faith. I need hardly say that, had I been aware that Republican messages were being broadcast from my lavatory I should have taken steps to see that the miscreants were brought to justice.

I am sorry to say that, (No doubt realizing the game was up) my daughter (who is no longer my daughter) and her paramour have made themselves scarce. It was not they who answered the door in the early hours of the morning to a burly squad of R.U.C. men; it was my wife Victoria Alberta (since admitted to hospital as a result of the shock to her nervous system). It was not they who were dragged from their beds in the early hours of the morning. It was I, Augustus Harland, Captain of the Boyne Protestant Defence Unit and founder member of the now defunct U.M.P.I.R.E. (a moderate Protestant organization).

I told them that I was a known Loyalist, and that it should be obvious to anyone with local knowledge that I would have no part in Republicanism or selling Ulster to the Pope.

They informed me that a number of Republican documents were suspected to be on my premises and that they were acting on information received from an elderly woman (Mother!!!) arrested for looting a public house on the Crumlin Road last night.

They then proceeded to search the house, with no success. However, one constable insisted on breaking the padlock on the outside lavatory, despite my insistence that it contained materials which were top secret, and the property of the Government Information Services.

Imagine my surprise when informed by the R.U.C. Sergeant that they were taking me in, on a charge under the Special Powers Act, under suspicion of operating an illegal radio transmitter. I may say that it was obvious from the papers and tapes found in the W.C. that my lavatory was, in fact, Radio Waterloo.

I am now placed in a very difficult position. If only my son Craig were here, he would advise me. I am being held in the Crumlin, and I have not been told what is to happen to me.

I am, at least, allowed to see newspapers, and I am happy to report that the R.C.s have been taught a lesson. The papers are, of course, not likely to report things as they actually happen. Republicans and Leftists on their Editorial Staff see to that. However I think the headline in this morning's *Newsletter* speaks for itself.

Boy (9) killed as bullets rake West Belfast
FIVE DIE IN AN ORGY OF SHOOTING

This is what the *Newsletter* has to say:

'Five people, including a nine year old boy, were shot dead and hundreds injured in a night which saw some of the most shameful street fighting in the history of Northern Ireland.'

(I should not call it shameful. I should call it a night of glory for true Loyalists!!!!! Aug. Harland.)

'Four of those fatally injured were killed in Belfast and the fifth in Armagh. Of 121 treated in hospital 42 were suffering from gunshot wounds. The total included 103 civilians and 18 police.'

(The Republicans will say they had no guns. Who then, shot our policemen? Perhaps R.C. policemen took advantage of the hubbub to shoot their Loyalist comrades? Aug. Harland.)

'The boy, Patrick Rooney, was killed when a bullet went through the window of his home in Brendan Pass, Divis Towers, and entered his head.

'One of the Belfastmen was killed when a bullet went through the window of his house and struck him. He was named as Mr Samuel McLarnon, aged 30, of Herbert Street, Crumlin Road. Another was Mr Herbert Roy, aged 26, of Hudson St., Belfast. Police said he was shot in the chest.

'The man who died in Armagh as a result of bullet wounds in the chest was named as Mr John Gallagher of Banbrook Hill, aged 20, and the father of three children.

'Another man was killed on the top of a block of flats in Divis Street. His body lay for some time before it could be brought down.

'In Armagh, the trouble broke out after a civil rights meeting in the town. A man who was injured and taken to hospital with gunshot wounds was named as Gerry Moore, aged 20, of Railway Street.

'In Belfast, fierce street fighting broke out shortly after 10 p.m. From then until the early hours of this morning the rattle of machine gun fire echoed through the Falls Road, Shankill Road, Crumlin Road, and surrounding Streets.

'Early this morning Hastings Street police Barracks and a nearby Roman Catholic Church were under severe attack.

Fierce Clashes

'Fierce clashes between Protestants and Roman Catholics broke out in Dover Street and Percy Street between the Shankill Road and the Falls Road.

'Armoured cars with machine guns mounted drove through streets which were littered with blazing petrol bombs.

'People in the Divis Towers flats and nearby houses on the Falls Road watched from unlit windows, dodging when gunfire broke out as the police cars raced down the street. Blazing buildings in the side streets lit the sky with an angry glow.

'A *Newsletter* photographer and reporter narrowly escaped injury when a burst from a machine gun hit the wall of the Divis Flats where they were sheltering.

'A stream of ambulances dealt with casualties and tension rose as reports of fatal injuries circulated. People who had been in the area earlier in the evening were trapped and afraid to venture out on the streets to go home.

'The trouble area expanded, spreading down to Castle Street, on to the Grosvenor Road and a cordon of people stretched across the Boyne Bridge at Sandy Row, blocking off the street.

'Dover Street itself was the scene of some of the worst

fighting since rioting began in Northern Ireland.

'Several constables, including some Specials, were injured, and three civilians were badly hurt.

'One man lying on the pavement had had his head battered and had lost an eye. Another was given treatment in a house in Cumberland Street. A third lay in the road waiting for an ambulance.

'Violence broke out at 10.30 p.m. when a group came into Dover Street from the Falls Road direction. Dover Street had so far been riot free although its population is half Protestant and half Roman Catholic.

'Constable Con Little had both his legs injured by stones and was unable to walk.

'Petrol bombs were thrown by both factions and the street was ablaze with flames. The Gaelic Hall was set on fire and when the fire brigade tried to get through their way was blocked for some time by a cordon across the street.

'After midnight firemen were still trying to get the blaze under control.

'Four armoured cars forced their way through the crowds, their sten guns revolving in the turrets.

'Several people were evacuated from their homes as the flames grew in intensity.

'Mrs Freda Connolly, shaking with fear and with tears streaming down her face, carried her 10 month old baby Rosalie, to safety.

'The major battle developed from hand to hand fighting in side streets.

'Both factions threw petrol bombs, bricks, iron bars and wooden cudgels and some of the more courageous met face to face in hand to hand combat. There were no signs of police interference at midnight.

'Organization seemed to be better from the Falls Road end as groups split up into pairs to carry milk crates of petrol bombs to their front line colleagues.

'There was almost continuous automatic gun fire and

rifle shots on the Falls Road, and R.U.C. H.Q. said at 1-30 a.m. that the police had been under tommy gun fire from the rioters who had earlier attacked Hastings Street police station.

'The police and Special Constabulary returned the fire, and bullets were whizzing through the air and ricocheting off buildings as people ran wildly for shelter.

'Violence also flared in the Hooker St.-Disraeli Street area, with Edenderry Arms licensed premises at Hooker St. ablaze and another public house at the corner of Disraeli Street burning.

'Fire bombs were hurled into book-makers premises in the area, and the noise of automatic weapons could be heard in the darkness of the side streets.

'Ten petrol bombs were thrown at the Royal Courts of Justice in Belfast, but no damage was done.

'It was reported that one young man who was shot on the Falls Road later received the last rites from a Priest.

'Early this morning, crowds had gathered on Newtownards Road.

'The trouble broke out in Armagh early last night when a crowd of 400 civil rights supporters had come out from the city hall following a public meeting.

'The stone throwing broke out between them and a group of Protestants who were grouped in the Upper English Street area, adjacent to the G.P.O. Riot police with shields and Specials carrying rifles baton charged civil rights supporters into the Nationalist Shambles area.

'Cheering Protestants followed the police as they drove the civil rights supporters again and again back into the Shambles area.

'Several windows were smashed by stones as the Protestants ran back towards the G.P.O.

'A car in the Shambles area was overturned and set alight by the rioters and running battles with the police were continuing into the early hours of this morning.

'Early this morning the police had contained civil rights supporters in Banbrook and Specials contained the Protestants near the City Hall, establishing a No Man's Land of about 100 yards.'

Explanatory Notes

These notes are intended to relate to the situation in August 1969. There have been many changes since but they do not materially alter the story. The political unit known as *'Northern Ireland'* consists of six of the nine counties of the province of *Ulster*. The remaining three counties, with the provinces of Munster, Leinster and Connaught, form the *Republic of Ireland*. The Government of the Republic of Ireland lays claim to the six northern counties as part of the land of Ireland, and the political group in the north known as *Republicans* reject the authority of *Northern Ireland Government* at *Stormont*. Roughly two thirds of the population of Northern Ireland is Protestant, whilst ninety-five per cent of the population of the Republic is Roman Catholic. The original intention of the British Government was to establish a 32 county state, with a parliament based on Dublin. The Protestants resisted this, as they feared Roman Catholic domination. Powerful leaders, *Carson* and *Craig*, with the backing of Protestant institutions such as the *Orange Order* succeeded in thwarting this intention, and the six counties became a separate political unit. The relationship between the *Stormont Parliament* and the parliament at *Westminster* is similar to the relationship between a state legislature and the Federal government, and interference by Westminster in Northern Ireland affairs is often the subject of controversy. Northern Ireland returns 12 M.P.s to Westminster, and these are usually Conservatives. The elections for the two parliaments are entirely separate. The Protestant majority party is known by the title of *Unionists*, and stands as the Conservative and Unionist Party. Those who believe in a thirty-two county Ireland but are prepared to work for it through the Stormont parliament make up the *Nationalist* party. The Northern Ireland Labour Party accepts the Stormont Parliament, and follows policy lines similar to the British Labour Party. The *Republican Labour Party* wishes for a thirty-two county state run on socialist lines, but is prepared to work through Stormont, despite the Republican label. The *Peoples Democracy* began as a student group at Queens University, but its influence and membership grew rapidly outside the confines of the University. It has a radical socialist philosophy. The *Civil Rights Association* contains people from all opposition groups. It was, and is, regarded by many Unionists as a Republican and/or Roman Catholic and/or Communist front organization; these widely divergent terms being seen as synonymous. It is doubtful if the C.R.A. has ever been the exclusive tool of any political grouping. The Unionist party itself embraces a wide spectrum of political opinion, drawn together by the idea of maintaining the union with Britain, more or less at all costs. Some Unionists would go so far as to fight the British, in order to stay British! The policies and personalities in both camps are so localized, that at times every individual seems to constitute a little party of his own. The campaign waged by the C.R.A. ... the Civil Rights Movement ... was not directed at the question of partition. Its main platform was, and is, discrimination against the Catholic minority by the Unionist Administration at all levels. However, so many of its spokesmen are identified with opposition to the border, that it became regarded as anti-partitionist. It should be realized that almost any Protestant/Catholic issue in the North is seen in these terms by many people on both sides, although many Roman Catholics favour partition, and many Protestants would favour its abolition. The *Irish Republican Army* is an illegal organization in both states, which aims to overthrow the state of Northern Ireland by force. Its campaign has fallen off of late, but the I.R.A. remains a potential menace, and is used by Unionist hard liners at every opportunity as a convenient bogeyman. The *U.V.F.*, or *Ulster Volunteer Force*, is its Protestant equivalent, also illegal. The *Royal Ulster Constabulary* is augmented by the *'B' Special Constabulary* (now disbanded). The 'B' Specials were an almost wholly Protestant force, armed, and regarded by many as the private army of the Unionist administration. The *Ulster Constitution Defence Committee* is composed of ardent 'Loyalists' and takes its inspiration from the Reverend Ian Paisley, who provides a rallying point for militant Protestants in his *Free Presbyterian Church* (The Free Presbyterians have no connection with the Presbyterian Church). This outline is grossly oversimplified, and not intended in any way to be regarded as definitive.

Places

Belfast is the chief city of Northern Ireland, upon which the parliament at *Stormont* is based. Of the major troubled areas mentioned, the *Shankhill Road* is Protestant, *Falls Road* Roman Catholic and the *Crumlin* a heady mixture of the two. *Newry* is a mainly Nationalist town, close to the border. *Londonderry* or *Derry* is a city with a two thirds Roman Catholic majority, carefully gerrymandered to produce a Unionist administration. Derry lost its hinterland as a result of partition, and has a high rate of unemployment, coupled with bad housing conditions. The *Bogside* is a Roman Catholic area in Derry. *Dublin* is the capital city of the Republic of Ireland. *Burntollet Bridge*, close to Derry, was the scene of a brutal assault by Protestant militants upon marching students. It is noteworthy that rioting took place almost exclusively in the 'slum' areas. Residential Belfast, for instance, went almost untouched.

People

Major James Chichester-Clark. Prime Minister of Northern Ireland (that is, of the Stormont Unionist administration). He replaced Captain Terence O'Neill, and it was believed that he would take a firmer line with opposition to Unionism. In the event, it seems apparent that the change in personalities did not bring about a change in policy.

Ivan Cooper. A Derry Protestant supporter of Civil Rights, a Stormont M.P., and henchman of Mr John Hume. Regarded as a 'traitor' by many Protestants.

William Craig. Former Minister of Home Affairs at Stormont, sacked by Captain Terence O'Neill. A leader of the extreme right of the Unionist Party, deeply mistrusted by the opposition.

Bernadette Devlin. Westminster M.P. for mid-Ulster, a product of the People's Democracy, and a fierce fighter for Civil Rights. Miss Devlin's youth and energy made a great impact in England, but at home her ardent socialism was mistrusted by many. Undoubtedly the outstanding 'romantic figure' of the whole episode, yet often the creature of her own passionate convictions.

Patrick (Paddy) Devlin. A very active Stormont M.P. for the Northern Ireland Labour Party, a keen supporter of the cause of Civil Rights.

Michael Farrell. An ardent Socialist, and one of the leaders of the Peoples Democracy.

Gerard Fitt. A Republican Labour M.P. at Westminster, he also holds a Stormont seat, and is a member of Belfast Corporation. Something of a political animal,

Mr Fitt works very hard at being Mr Fitt ... and does a lot of good work in the process!

John Hume. A Stormont M.P., and to my mind the outstanding figure in the fight for Civil Rights. Mr Hume is disliked by the militants on his own side, and hated by the Unionists. He is a Roman Catholic, and his work in Derry with Mr Ivan Cooper has made many people look to him as a leader for the future. All this being so, it is an illustration of the absurdity of Northern Ireland Politics that Mr Hume obtained his Stormont seat by defeating the Leader of the Nationalist Party, Mr Edward McAteer, also a sane politician ... of which we haven't got many! The candidate who finished third in this particular election was yet another prominent supporter of Civil Rights, Mr Eamonn McCann, self styled revolutionary. These three could all have been usefully employed in Stormont by the Civil Rights Movement, though Mr McCann might well have blown the place up ... verbally!

Jack Lynch. Prime Minister of the Republic. His Fianna Fail party, while backing the Civil Rights Movement in the North, had in hand legislation of its own to which the Peoples Democracy ... rightly ... took strong exception. In other circumstances, his government and that of James Chichester-Clark would have much in common.

Captain Terence O'Neill. Regarded as a 'liberal' Unionist, his vague gestures towards the Catholic minority brought a hornets nest of Protestants round his ears. He did his best, but he couldn't beat his own party.

Reverend Ian Paisley. A militant Protestant cleric, a powerful orator, a man who sees himself as the defender of the Protestant faith against all and sundry.

Robert Porter. Minister of Home Affairs at Stormont, distrusted by militant Unionists. His position is probably similar to Captain O'Neill's.

Harold Wilson. As Prime Minister of Great Britain, was deeply distrusted by the Unionists, who believe that the British Labour Party is less likely to favour their cause than the Conservative and Unionist Party. This belief is founded both upon history and upon the fact that the Unionists habitually co-operate with the Conservatives, and their ten (sometimes twelve) votes have from time to time proved a grave embarrassment to the Labour Government. While this is true, Ireland is the traditional graveyard of English politicians, and the Labour Party has never shown itself particularly anxious to become involved in Northern Ireland's affairs.